THE CHRONICLES OF

BLARNIA

THE CHRONICLES OF
BLARNIA

The Lying Bitch in the Wardrobe

MICHAEL GERBER

A Story for the Childish

The right of Michael Gerber to be identified as the
author of this work has been asserted by him in accordance
with the Copyright, Designs and Patents Act 1988.

First published in Great Britain in 2005 by
Gollancz
An imprint of the Orion Publishing Group
Orion House, 5 Upper St Martin's Lane,
London WC2H 9EA

A CIP catalogue record for this book
is available from the British Library

ISBN-13 978 0 575 07816 1
ISBN-10 0 575 07816 2

1 3 5 7 9 10 8 6 4 2

Typeset at The Spartan Press Ltd,
Lymington, Hants

Printed in Great Britain by
Clays Ltd, St Ives plc

The Orion Publishing Group's policy is to use papers that
are natural, renewable and recyclable products and
made from wood grown in sustainable forests. The logging
and manufacturing processes are expected to conform to
the environmental regulations of the country of origin.

www.orionbooks.co.uk

To Giacomo Parodista
(1471–1517; 1518)
History's first parodist and the only
man to be burned at the stake *twice*.

'The best way to drive out the devil,
if he will not yield to texts of scripture, is to
jeer and flout him, for he cannot bear scorn.'
– *Martin Luther, as quoted by C.S. Lewis*

'The devil can cite Scripture for his purpose.'
The Merchant of Venice, Act I, Scene 3.

A Note to Parents and
Other Concerned Parties:

With the flood of offensive material constantly being produced by irresponsible people only interested in making a quick buck,[1] it is nearly impossible to monitor what today's young people are being exposed to. That is why this book has been printed using a new process I've invented called 'CensorVision.'

CensorVision renders offensive materials COM-PLETELY INVISIBLE to the uncorrupted eye. If the reader has not already read, heard, or thought about one of the words in this book, that word will not appear, leaving instead a harmless blank space.

Here's an example. The following sentence contains several extremely shocking, but largely unknown, profanities. 'It was ____, _____, _____-_____ dark and stormy night.' Thanks to CensorVision, this should read as a thoroughly insipid – but *completely harmless* – sentence. If it does not, please return your copy of the book immediately as your CensorVision unit is defective and may explode at any moment. Either

[1] Hi there!

that, or you are an incredibly depraved individual in need of professional help. In which case, join the club.

Thanks for reading, and I hope you enjoy the story. It's totally _____, and just filled with _____ and ____ and _____. There's even a little _____, right at the very end. It will blow your _____ mind! My _____ computer busted, it was so _____ dirty!

Either that, or it's a lovely, quite morally instructive story about four plucky English schoolkids.

CHAPTER 1

Once there were four children named Pete, Sue, Ed and Loo, and this story is about something that happened to them when their parents sold them for medical experiments. Well, *rented* them, actually – we must be fair.

Early one morning, quite against their will, Pete, Sue, Ed, and Loo were carefully packaged up in brown paper and delivered to the house of an old Professor. The Professor, who had purchased his credentials over the Internet, lived in the absolute arse-end of the country, ten long miles from the nearest police station – and there was a very good reason for this. Some of the things that went on in the house were somewhat shady, but scientific progress can be like that. The Professor had no wife, which was a bit of a giveaway, and lived in a large, heavily guarded mansion with a housekeeper named Mrs MacBeth and several servants, each of whom were much too low-class to figure in the story, or even have proper names. Don't worry, I won't mention them again.

The Professor had white hair and large, frightening

muttonchop whiskers that the children had only seen once before, in terrifying pictures of Isaac Asimov. He wore a white lab coat and carried a stethoscope which he used constantly, even on things like tables and chairs. When the Professor came to the front door to unwrap and frisk them, the four Perversie children felt an urge to flee, like their insides were filled with wriggling bubbles. But it seemed impolite to run, especially since the charwomen had Uzis under their aprons.

So there they stood in the grand front hall of the house as Mrs MacBeth clipped their twine and removed their postage (in Ed's case plucking out part of an eyebrow in the process). When they were all unwrapped the Professor checked their teeth and gave a satisfied grunt. Even though none of the children had ever been to Sweden, all of them immediately developed Stockholm Syndrome, liking and trusting their captor the Professor implicitly – all of them, that is, except the youngest boy, Ed.

Ed was the smartest of the Perversie children, and he suffered as a result. His brother Pete was more or less permanently concussed from absorbing too many cricket balls squarely on the forehead. His sister Sue's brain was average, not to mention relatively undamaged; but the girl considered unconventional thoughts to be marks against one's character, and so was incredibly, drive-a-fork-into-your-own-eye boring.

As for the runt of the litter, poor chittering, confused Loo – nobody knew exactly what was wrong with her. She was constantly getting into trouble; one doctor had, by way of ending the appointment, called the girl 'a genius of self-annihilation.' As the only one with a smidgeon of responsibility, Sue had her hands full trying to keep Loo from accidentally poisoning, asphyxiating, crushing, immolating, or otherwise destroying herself. Some days, it was hard not to think she had the right idea – like right now, for example. Within moments of entering the Professor's house Loo had clambered onto a table and was vainly trying to suckle at the nozzle of a disconnected Victorian-era gaslight.

Ed watched her dispassionately. 'Memo to myself,' he said into his upraised index finger, 're: Loo's behaviour.' Ed Perversie was determined to become rich and powerful someday. The first step, for him, was to get a portable voice recorder, so as not to forget all the brilliant ideas and observations that flowed out of him every single day. This seemed to Ed to be a completely reasonable request, but when he had asked his parents to buy him one, they had stared at him uncomprehendingly. This was just more proof, Ed felt, that Mr and Mrs Perversie were idiots consigned to a life of poverty and squalor. Ed went back and forth as to whether he would support them in their old age. He probably *would*, just to teach them a lesson.

Undaunted, Ed was determined to cultivate the habit anyway, and so it was common to find the boy dictating can't-miss schemes and sterling insights regarding Life's Rich Pageant into his upraised right index finger. 'Is Loo's behaviour a cry for help? Or is it,' Ed said this time, 'merely a cry for a pounding?'

Ed's opinions aside, it is doubtful that even Loo understood the forces that drove her to – taking one of the less colorful examples – spend a lovely mid-summer's afternoon trying to flatten herself to death with Mum's rolling pin. Children are not any less mysterious than adults, they simply have it all packed into a smaller space.

Pete spotted his brother leaving himself a memo. Even though Ed had explained the process many times, Pete asked, 'What are you doing, fishing for bogeys?'

Ed gave a sneer; like Eskimos and their many words for snow, Ed had an entire repertoire of facial expressions designed to convey negative emotions to his siblings. I know you may find this hard to believe, dear reader, but Ed had the misfortune of being born into a family of enormous boobs.[2] Such a thing is very nearly unheard of, as I'm sure you know, for most siblings are the bestest chums in the whole world. You yourself, for instance, are undoubtedly so fond of your brothers and sisters that you often simply cannot *stand* how keen you are on them. I bet you occasionally pinch yourself and box your own ears, simply from the pure joy of it.

But poor Ed was not so lucky. In addition to pulling faces he busied himself with tormenting the others whenever and however he could. His siblings were never able to penetrate his diabolical cunning, and as a result the other Perversie children were quite super-stitious believing (for example) that evil elves began each day by urinating on their cereal. Uncanny hap-penings like that were only too easy to believe, now that they were in a creepy old house far off in the country, filled with strange people, some of whom surely had extensive criminal records.

After filling out hours of paperwork, made even longer by bickering (Sue couldn't believe that 'inden-tured servitude' meant what Ed said it did, it seemed so *unfair*), the children had been sent to bed.

---

[2] Oh, get your mind out of the gutter, would you? There's only room for one, and I got here first.

'No supper tonight,' Professor Berke told them, 'so the testing can begin bright and early tomorrow.'

As soon as they had turned in for the evening, the boys crept over to the girls' room to explicate the plot.

'This place is absolutely spiffing!' Pete yelled, bursting into the room. 'No parents for miles! We can do whatever we want!' Unfortunately, what Pete wanted to do was act like he always did, hyper and destructive. Pillow cradled under his arm like a rugby ball, Pete darted around the room barrelling into this and that.

'Testosterone poisoning,' Ed muttered, dodging a toppling coat stand. 'Who else thinks the Professor's one of Amnesty International's Ten Most Wanted?' he asked.

'Oh, he's not as bad as all that,' his older sister Sue said gently. 'I think he's an old dear.'

'Well, *obviously*,' Ed said. 'Wait – did you just say "dear"?'

Sue frowned at the off-colour remark. She frowned at everything – Sue was that type of child, super-serious without the usual adult excuses like unpaid taxes or a difficult menopause. They all jumped as Pete crashed into a dresser, knocking himself unconscious. It was hard to talk with Pete around.

'Criminal or not, this Professor's bloody cheap,' Ed harrumphed. 'Making us pay our own postage . . .'

'I think he's awfully nice to take us in,' Loo chimed

in, 'what with the Germans invisi-bombing London.'
She examined a book, then rather tentatively attempted
to close it over her windpipe. It didn't work.

'*Invisi*-bombing, right,' Ed said. Loo would believe
anything. Usually Ed delighted in gaslighting her, but
at the moment he was too irritated. 'Look — I explained
this in the back of the Royal Mail van up from London.
There is no War . . .'

Pete came awake. 'Did somebody say "war"?' he
said, raring to go.

'. . . World War Two ended decades ago. Mum and
Dad are *lying*.'

'Oh, pish,' Sue chided. 'Don't be ridiculous. If there
was no War, why would they make us wear helmets in
the shower?'

'The same reason Dad pretended his arm was blown
off by a bomb.'

'Now you're just being silly,' Loo said. 'Didn't you
see it that morning at breakfast? Before it grew back?'

'Arms don't grow back,' Ed said. 'He just stuck it
inside his shirt – like this.' He demonstrated, then
pulled it out.

'It's another miracle! Twice in the same family!' Loo
exclaimed, then shot Ed a dirty look. 'And *you* think it's
stupid to go to church.'

Sue sat with her hands in her lap and her brow

knitted. Ed was beginning to win her over – her natural darkness of aspect made it easy for her to expect sharp dealings.[3] 'But Ed, why would they lie to us? Are you saying Mum and Dad – our very own flesh and blood – are *Srebnian*?'

'I'm saying they're nutters,' Ed said dispassionately. 'They sold our cat. Or do you still believe it ran off to "make a go of it in Hollywood"?'

'Look here, Perversie Minor!' Pete said, dropping the pillow and balling his fists. 'I don't let anybody talk about my parents that way!' He dropped into a crouch and approached Ed. 'Put 'em up!' he said, whirling his fists like an old-time pugilist.

Ed pulled some pepper spray from his pocket and gave his brother a generous squirt. As Pete windmilled around the room howling, Ed handed Sue a scrap of paper. 'I found this classified ad in Dad's dresser.'

---

[3] Especially if Srebnians were involved. For some reason, Sue believed this mildest of all peoples was responsible for most of the world's troubles. In fact, to her, bad behaviour of any kind was an infallible indicator of hidden Srebnian heritage. It was sad to see someone so crippled by prejudice. Ed had signed Sue up for newsletters from various Srebnian governmental groups; for some reason, she was particularly enraged by material from the Srebnian national soccer team. 'It's because they pretend to be harmless . . .' Sue said.

'You go through Dad's dresser?' Loo gasped, as if she had expected the pure naughtiness of this to strike Ed dead. 'I'm telling!'

'Quiet, Loo.' Sue took the paper and read it. 'Calling All Parents!' she read aloud. 'Rent Me Your Children for £OADS of £O££Y!'

Pete bellowed incoherently, hands scrabbling at his eyes. He had to be sprayed several times a day simply to be kept in line, so no one paid much attention to his noisy thrashings. He slammed into a bookcase and pulled it down with a crash.

'Pete, please do control yourself, I'm trying to read.'

'Sorry,' Pete said, eyes streaming. He tucked his head into his armpit, and screamed into his shirt.

' "Tired of your offspring? Let me take them off your hands for one month – six months – you name it!" ' Sue read. 'Rogue chemist in quaint, paramilitary style compound seeks human subjects to test next gen-eration of hormone therapies. Largest independent live-tester in UK. Subjects must be prepubescent and/ or easily subdued. Extreme gullibility a plus. No child too weeny – let's make a deal!" ' Sue let it sink in, then handed the scrap to her younger sister. Loo refused to take it.

'No! I don't care what you say!' Loo said, crumpling up the scrap and throwing it at Ed. 'There *is* a war, and the Professor *is* a tenured academic, and . . . and . . . Papa wouldn't do that to us!' cried Loo despairingly.

Pete, Sue and Ed looked at Loo, all thinking the same thing. Loo loved their father desperately, so no one ever mentioned that she looked strikingly like the Pakistani man who owned the tobacconist's at the end of the road.

'There, there, Loo, there, there,' Sue said maternally, comforting her younger sister with a quick sleeper hold. As Loo slumped to the floor, Sue said, 'She'll be quiet for a bit. Pete, you're the oldest, what do you think we should do?'

'Hey!' Ed said. 'I was the one who—'

'Ed's right,' Pete said, still red-eyed but calm. Pete's incredible recuperative powers made Ed suspect he was a mutant. 'So, Ed, what should we do?'

'Escape, obviously. And even more obviously, not drink or eat anything until then. It'll probably have drugs in it.'

'Right,' Pete said decisively. 'If we're going to escape, we need to find a pommel horse.'

'Ooh, a horse!' Loo loved horses almost as much as she loved the icy embrace of the Beyond. 'After we find it, can I keep it?'

'Loo, aren't you unconscious?'

'Oops, I forgot,' Loo said, in the first of many logical

mistakes in this story. Ed shook his head; it was going to be one of *those* books. Meanwhile, back in the narrative, Sue looked concerned.

'What's wrong, Sue?' Pete asked.

'Pete, I know you're . . . sporty,' Sue said, 'but do you really think gymnastics are appropriate at this juncture?'

Pete laughed brightly. 'No, no, Sue – that's how we're going to get out of here! We'll move the pommel horse out on the lawn, and take turns crouching underneath it, digging a tunnel, carrying the dirt out in our pants. I saw it in a film.'

Ed turned to Pete. 'I cannot believe I am related to you,' he said.

'Well, what's your brilliant idea?'

'I don't know – running, perhaps? I know that's awfully common, but . . .'

'No, no, we couldn't do that,' Sue said. 'I haven't written a thank-you note.'

'Oh, for God's sake!' Ed cried.

Sue was implacable. 'When you stay at someone's home—'

'Against your will?'

'—a thank-you note is customary,' Sue said. 'I haven't even got any nice stationery.'

Ed was silent, looking out the window at the moon

which cast a mocking reflection on the moat below. Trying to pour oil on troubled waters, Pete asked, 'Ed, what are you thinking?'

'I'm thinking, "If I pushed Sue out of this window, would she ruin everything by surviving?"'

'Ed!' Sue yelled sotto voce. 'Shut up! You'll give you-know-who ideas.'

'I already had that idea,' Loo interjected. 'Is that a moat? I thought it was a circular river.'

'Yes, it is a moat, Loo, and you are not to die in it,' Sue said, slamming the window shut. She scowled in Ed's direction. They each pulled out concealed knives and began circling each other. Sue had learned knife-fighting in the Girl Guides, Ed in the Boy Scouts (before he got kicked out for insubordination).

Pete, the natural leader, stepped in. 'Ed – Sue – we've got to stick together, especially if it's as bad as Ed seems to think it is.'

Ed looked up from his shiv. 'What do you mean, "seems to think"? Maybe you're looking forward to being vivisected—'

'Mr Gloom-and-Doom,' Sue said, retracting her stiletto. 'We might just get cosmetics squirted into our eyes.'

'Great! I'll be sure to write a thank-you note.'

'Look Ed, I know you're annoyed that we're not

using your escape plan,' Pete said, 'but I just feel it's a bit . . . risky. The sooner we find a pommel horse —'

'And some stationery,' Sue piped up.

'—right, and some stationery, the sooner we'll be back home.'

'With our parents, the dangerous psychotics,' Ed said.

Pete bristled at the insult, then remembered the pepper spray. 'I'll let that one go, since we're related,' he said. 'If it's fine tomorrow, we'll put up the pommel horse and start digging.'

The next day was an English summer classic – dreary and wet. The clammy, strangely adhesive fog was so thick that when you looked out the window you couldn't see the mountains nor the woods, nor even the garden where the German Shepherds were starved to make them more vicious.

Ed looked out the window – it was perfect! Usually Ed liked to wake up early and listen to whatever his brother was mumbling in his sleep, on the chance it was off-colour and embarrassing. Today, however, there wasn't time.

'Pete, wake up,' Ed said, shaking his brother.

'Top-hole . . . Head Boy . . . beastliness . . .' Pete mumbled.

Ed shook more vigorously. 'Wake up, you clod! We have to go!'

Pete sat up, and rubbed the sleep from his eyes.

'Hurry up and dress!' Ed said, throwing Pete his school uniform.[4] 'There's fog on the ground – if we can just get into the woods . . .'

'No, Ed,' Pete said resolutely. 'I promised Sue she'd be able to write a thank-you note.' Pete's word was his bond, no matter how stupid that word turned out to be.

Ed fell back, flipped over and screamed long and loud into his pillow, kicking his feet wildly with frustration.

'Don't worry,' Pete said, clapping his younger brother on the back. 'It'll be a piece of cake. I'm sure there's a pommel horse around here somewhere. And you know what they say: where there's a pommel horse, there's always notepaper.'

---

[4] A combination of idiocy and straitened circumstances had meant that Pete had been rejected by every public school in the country. He eventually made it into a dog obedience school, only to be turned away when he arrived at 'start-of-term' with his trunk, boater, and tennis racquet. Ever since then, Pete had lived in a fantasy world. Fearing the inevitable social repercussions of a brother on a multi-state killing spree, upon Pete's return Sue had sewn him a 'school uniform,' complete with a crest made of crossed bones over a hydrant.

'They say that, do they? Do they also say, "Get ready to be buggered by a mad scientist because your parents leased you out like a spare bedroom?'

Pete looked thoughtful. 'No,' he said. 'No, I don't think they say that.'

'Well, you're going to.'

Before they could look for the escaping equipment, the children had to have breakfast with their 'bene-factor' in the gloomy dining room downstairs. This was not very pleasant, as the Perversies were determined not to eat or drink anything, and the Professor was equally determined to start his experimentation. As the Professor's face grew darker and darker, the children kept spilling and dropping things, which Mrs MacBeth would dutifully replace. When they were all ankle-deep in shards and food, the Professor admitted defeat.

'So we'll do it the hard way,' he said. The Professor threw down his napkin and marched out.

'I hope we did the right thing,' Sue said. 'The Professor seemed quite cross.'

'I think we did,' Pete piped up. He pointed at a once-normal houseplant. 'I poured my milk on it.' The plant was now growing sideways.

'I'm *so* out of here,' Ed said. He got up and began stretching out his hamstrings in preparation for the sprint to come.

'Ed, wait,' Sue said. 'What shall we do when we find the pommel horse?'

'Oh, you're still stuck on that,' Ed grumbled. 'I was hoping a good night's sleep had pounded the merest fragment of sense into your noggin. Now I see how ridiculously optimistic that was.'

'I suppose we'll need a signal of some sort,' Pete said.

'How about shouting, "Hey, sods, I bloody found the bleeding —'

'Ed!' Sue scolded, clapping her hands over Loo's ears.

'Too late!' Loo sang happily. 'I've heard it all before anyway. You have no idea how rough it is, out on the playground,' she said, with a touch of world-weariness.

'How about a bird call?' Pete suggested. 'I'll do an eagle. Sue, you can be a dove, Ed, you can be an owl, and Loo – Loo, do you know any bird calls?'

'How about a chicken?' Ed offered. He knew such talk was spiteful, but since the alternative was suffocating them all in their beds, he was actually being quite virtuous.

'That'll have to do,' Pete said. 'Now, if anybody stops you, say you're looking for a bathroom. Ed, are you listening?'

'No.'

'Good,' Pete said, not listening either. 'Let's get started.'

Detemined to cover more ground and add drama to the plot, the children split up. Though the house's great age meant that whole wings of it were constantly collapsing into so much dust, the manor was still immense. When the upkeep on it became too steep, the Professor had tried to give it to the government, but they had refused. Cursing the high cost of dynamite, he opened the pile to tourists; within six months of doing so he had saved up such a reservoir of distaste for his fellow man that converting his ancestral home into a heavily guarded outpost of quasi-medical torture seemed only logical. He, like Ed, was a man of great passions – if by 'passions' one means a capacity for annoyance.

The manor was a warren of wood-panelled passageways, lined with over-dark paintings of illustrious ancestors. (Each of the Professor's antecedents sported luxurious muttonchop whiskers, even the women.) Every so often, much to Pete's excitement, there was a suit of armour; it was invariably pierced and/or dented in painful ways, signalling that the Professor's ancestors were either hopeless fighters or shameless corpsepickers.

The manor's layout was sprinkled with funny little passageways and stairways leading nowhere – and every third door opened on to a brick wall bearing the message, 'Psych!' It was certainly the strangest house the children had ever seen, and the dustiest: Professor Berke's housekeeper Mrs MacBeth really didn't have time, preoccupied as she was with washing gobs of invisible blood off her hands.

No one had bothered to explain to Loo what a pommel horse was, so the image she kept in mind as she trundled from room to room was of the diarrhetic and bitey Shetland pony she had ridden last summer. It was amazing how a piece of old furniture covered with a sheet could look slightly horse-like, at least to an eight-year-old weak from hunger. After five rooms filled with nothing but mildew and disappointment, Loo was having trouble concentrating over the rumble of her empty stomach.

The next room Loo tried seemed to be empty except for a large wardrobe. It was an ordinary room, no different than the five before . . . yet Loo lingered. As her eyes adjusted to the gloom, she also saw a rabbit hole, a looking glass, Platform $9\frac{3}{4}$, and, lying in the corner, a small tesseract. Loo reckoned the wardrobe was just big enough for a pony standing on its hind legs . . . The door opened quite easily, almost as if she had been meant to step inside.

She entered, taking care to leave the door slightly

ajar. Loo knew it was foolish to lock oneself inside a wardrobe, but as Ed was fond of saying, 'Foolish things are Loo's business.' Just in the last year, she had climbed into an abandoned refrigerator, lowered herself into a well, and even stowed away in the wheel well of an aeroplane bound for the Dutch East Indies. Getting stuck in stink-wreathed portable toilets was a particular speciality, which inspired Ed to give her the nickname 'Loo.'

Inside the wardrobe, Loo looked around. The crack of light revealed not a horse, but the wildest clothes Loo had ever seen. It was hippie regalia of the highest order: satin Sergeant Pepper-style jackets, beaded vests, capes of black velvet and psychedelic paisley. She examined a satin jacket, rummaged through the pockets, and found a sugar lump.

'Brilliant!' Loo said quietly. Where there were sugar lumps, there were often ponies. Loo parted the clothes and went deeper. 'He must be around here somewhere,' she thought, stretching her hands out so as not to run into him. 'Here, pony, pony, pony . . .' Loo said softly. 'If you don't come out, I'll eat your sugar lump . . .' Loo said. She waited two seconds, listening hard for a whinny or sounds of gastric distress. Hearing neither, she popped the lump into her mouth. Presently she was glad to have done it; the tiny morsel of food made her feel better.

What an enormous wardrobe, Loo thought, as the walls began to wobble and flex. Her foot bumped into something hard, and she reached down to see what it was. It was a large bottle of brown glass with a yellowed label that Loo could barely make out: '1000x Banana-Peel Extract , Eel Pie Island Hotel, ca. 1966.' Then, underneath, in shaky pen: 'Warning: Extremely Powerful, Man.' As she was looking at the label, the bottle turned into a hedgehog wearing a bowler, and Loo put it down gently.

'Sue always said we must be kind to animals,' Loo said aloud as the hedgehog skittered away, speaking French. She thought guiltily of the poor grasshopper Pete had pulled the legs off last week. She saw it clearly in her mind, mutilated, waving its stumps in the dust, screaming in a way human ears couldn't perceive. Should she have kept the hedgehog? Loo wondered. Maybe it would've come in handy. She couldn't remember whether hedgehogs were poisonous or not.

'What was I doing? Oh, right, looking for the pony.' Loo continued to walk. 'Here pony, pony, pony . . .' she called, noticing that the darkness inside the wardrobe was suddenly very B-flat minor.

All of a sudden Loo realized that what was brushing her hands and face weren't the natural fabrics and retro-Victorian fashions of Swinging London, but prickly evergreens. 'Oh wowwww,' Loo said, tripping heavily.

There seemed to be a light up ahead, which to Loo's scrambled brains clearly was God. She turned to run – if God was anything like Mum and Dad described Him, He was nobody she'd like to meet. But then she stumbled, and this gave her a chance to consider. He's everywhere *anyway*, and probably already knows about the grasshopper, Loo thought, so she might as well go and say hello.

In this Loo revealed herself to be a sensible girl (apart from her burning desire to snuff it). After all, how often does one get to meet the Almighty? He travels a great deal, and is very hard to reach under the best of circumstances.

Loo walked into the snow – *snow?* – and after ten steps found herself in a wood. Her courage failed again, just for a moment; but then she looked back and saw the crack of light from the open wardrobe door, far behind her. She had, in an uncharacteristic burst of sensibleness that we can safely chalk up to the drugs, left the wardrobe door ever so slightly open. (All children should know it is very foolish to shut yourself inside a wardrobe, and their parents should know that by buying books describing this they have automatically given up the right to sue the author, who in any case has extremely powerful legal representation.)

Reassured, Loo walked on. After ten minutes of walking, she realised that the light wasn't God, but an ordinary traffic light, flashing red-amber-green in the middle of the snowy woods. The girl's fried consciousness accepted this as the most natural thing in the world. She reached out and grooved on the cold metal. Just as she was about to lick it, Loo heard footsteps coming towards her.

At first glance, Loo thought it was the pony, walking on its hind legs. But as it approached through the scrim of snow, she realised that it was a much stranger creature than that – it appeared to be a goat, comporting itself like a man.

Hadn't Mum and Dad told her goats were Satanic? Or was she thinking of calico cats? She wrinkled her nose; whatever it was, the creature was definitely French. That explained the small pointed beard – but what about the little horns? Satan, definitely Satan. Satan was carrying several parcels, probably damned souls consigned to Hell. Loo felt her trip turning into a bummer, but was determined not to freak out. I'll hide behind this traffic light, she thought, and examine him further.

Distracted with his errands and the thickly falling

snow, the creature walked right by. As it passed, Loo saw something she'd never forget: while his front was that of a goat, covered in woolly hair, his entire rear side was that of a flabby, gray, middle-aged man! As Loo stared at his wobbling, pebbled buttocks in horror, she heard the creature mumble to himself.

'Oh, dear, oh dear!' He looked at his pocket watch. 'I shall be too late!'

Loo couldn't stop herself. Outraged, she stepped from behind the lamppost and yelled, 'Hey! That's from another book!'

When he saw Loo, the Faun was so surprised that a short stream of golden urine jetted into the snow. 'Holy Christ!' exclaimed the Faun, scattering parcels everywhere.

CHAPTER 2

 'Copyright infringement is no laughing matter,' Loo said as forcefully as a girl her age and stature could manage. 'Furthermore, you should be more careful with your packages. You never know when they might be children.'

The Faun looked puzzled.

'Sent to the country.' More confusion. 'Because of the War! The invisi-bombing – surely you've not seen it?' Loo said.

The Faun shrugged.

'You must've been speaking to my brother Ed,' Loo grumbled. 'I hate him.'

'No idea what you're nattering on about,' the Faun said, kicking over some snow to hide his accident. 'Anyway, I don't take orders from dandelions.'

Now it was Loo's turn to be confused.

'It's obvious: you're a dandelion,' the Faun said. He patted his head. 'Yellow on top.'

Loo opened and closed her mouth in amazement, then sputtered, 'I'm not a flower, I'm a girl!'

The Faun sniffed the cold winter air. 'Not bloody

likely! All my books say that girls are made of sugar and spice and everything nice. You, on the other hand, smell like a year-old carton of milk.'

Loo, who didn't much like showers, and quite often forgot to change her underpants, blushed fiercely. 'I am not a dairy product!' she mumbled. 'I'm a child! My name is Loo!'

'Are you a mobile phone, perhaps? They can do the most amazing things with technology.'

Loo, unused to being the smart one, stamped up and down in the snow. 'No! No! No! I'm a girl, a child, a human being!'

The Faun's eyes grew large. 'A Daughter of Steve? Truly?' Quite unexpectedly, he began to hum 'We're in the Money.'

'Daughter of who?' Loo asked.

'A Daughter of Steve, as in Atom and Steve. Strange that no females were involved, but it's your creation myth, not mine,' the Faun said. 'Still, Steve's not so bad. If you were from certain African tribes, I'd call you "Daughter of a Palm Nut."'

'Do I *look* African?' Loo asked.

'No need to get indignant,' the Faun said. 'I was just indulging in a little comparative religion – not everyone's taste to be sure, but harmless enough – drawing out the commonalities between people – the need of every group

Michael Gerber

to come up with a myth – and of course, it strikes others outside the group as absurd – I mean, a *rib*!'

Whatever this guy was on about, Loo didn't think her parents would approve. 'At least I don't go around with my bottom hanging out,' Loo cracked.

'Oh, here we go,' the Faun said, 'poking fun at the fact that I'm a vertical Faun, rather than a horizontal one. Do you think I wanted to be born this way?'

Embarrassed, Loo didn't know what to say. 'I think I hear my mother calling,' she finally said, and turned to go.

'No, no, Daughter of Steve, don't go!' the Faun said. 'Baby needs a new pair of shoes! I am a friend!' He hooked her arm with the handle of his umbrella. The casing slid off, revealing a sword. 'Ha! Ha! That's my poker! For rubbish!' He frantically poked a few stray leaves. 'I mean you no harm – just slide that back on there, thanks.'

Loo wasn't totally convinced. 'People who are friendly don't make comments about how other people smell,' she said. 'You don't smell very nice yourself.'

'I'm sorry. Please forgive me, O Loo, Daughter of Steve,' the Faun said, attempting to turn on the charm. 'I'm of greater than average intelligence, but my social skills leave much to be desired. Have you heard of Asperger's Syndrome?'

'No,' Loo said. Talking to the Faun was like walking in deep mud that sucked your Wellies off. 'Please don't take offence, sir, but I'm wondering if English is your first language.'

'Really? You don't read much, do you?' the Faun said. '*She* doesn't like it, either – that I'm very intelligent – *she* wants to keep me in my place. That's why they call me Mr Dumbness.'

'That's not very nice,' Loo said. 'My brother Ed calls me "Loo." He's never told me why.'

'Ah, the abuse of others,' the Faun said, extending his hoof. 'The surest glue of a fledgling friendship. Mr Dumbness, at your service.'

Loo shook his hoof. 'Pleased to meet you, Mr Dumbness.'

'How have you come to Blarnia?' Mr Dumbness said.

'Blarnia? Is that what the Professor's back garden is called?'

'This is all the land of Blarnia,' said the Faun. 'From the traffic light in the western woods to the great castle of Cair Amel on the eastern sea, bordered on the south by Oz, on the west by Middle Earth, and on the north by Made-upistan.'

'I— I got in through the wardrobe,' said Loo.

Mr Dumbness looked at her in disbelief. "You got

here through a wardrobe?" he asked. 'What are you, high?'

Loo didn't know how to respond to this. There was a moment of quiet. Mr Dumbness stood, idly tracing a pound sign in the snow with his cloven hoof.

'Well, I suppose I'd better go . . .' Loo said. 'I have to find a pommel horse . . .'

'Wait!' Mr Dumbness said. 'How about you and me go back to my place – for tea! And cake! That's all. No . . . abduction, or anything like that. Bwa ha ha ha!'

There was something in Mr Dumbness' evil laugh that Loo found deeply reassuring. 'What's an "abduction"?' she asked.

'I'll explain on the way,' Mr Dumbness said, tossing his parcels into a snowdrift and grabbing Loo by the arm. 'Tell me, are you made of equal parts sugar and spice, or does one predominate?'

The two walked through the wood, Mr Dumbness trying his best to counteract Loo's unerring instinct towards self-extinguishing. In the short distance to Mr Dumbness' home, Loo nearly fell off a cliff, tried unsuccessfully to wake a hibernating bear, and narrowly missed plunging into an abandoned silver mine. Finally, at the bottom of a small hollow, Mr Dumbness suddenly turned aside, as if he were going to walk straight into a large rock. Which he did. Woozy, he crawled aimlessly for ten feet or so, until he found a hidden entrance, just big enough for a small creature (or a girl) to squeeze through. 'I can never find it unless I'm slightly concussed,' Mr Dumbness admitted.

Inside, it was dry and cosy, with décor that was equal parts Oxford don and Biblical hermit. The cave had few luxuries except for dozens of bookcases and a small, steam-powered DVD player. There was a carpet on the floor and two little chairs.

'One for me,' said Mr Dumbness, 'and one for my prey. Uh, friend! I meant to say friend.'

'Thank you,' Loo said, taking a seat. Fully warmed now, her nose was assaulted by the close, brothy smell of the cave, the scent of someone half covered with hair who doesn't bathe. She suddenly realized how hungry she was, and wondered if it would be impolite to ask her host if he might shave a hoof and whip up some gelatin.

As Mr Dumbness prepared the tea, Loo kept catching uncomfortable glimpses of his bare bottom. Embarrassed, she turned to look at the books on Mr Dumbness' shelves. She pulled out one called 'Beyond Candy: Luring Today's Wised-Up Preteens,' but it didn't have any pictures. Then she tried 'Let's Put the "Kid" Back in Kidnapping,' but that was even more boring. Slipping the book back on to the shelf, Loo looked around. There was an oil painting of a bunch of Fauns playing poker.

'It's a cliche, I know,' Mr Dumbness said. 'But my father's in it – third from the left.'

'That's nice,' Loo said blandly. Then her eye strayed to a plaque on the wall reading 'Collaborator of the Month.'

Mr Dumbness gave a horrified look, then caught himself. 'That's just a little joke! The award – it's not real – it couldn't be, how could it? How silly! Ridiculous. Just a little, ridiculous, not-real 100% joke that my co-workers put together. As a joke.'

'Oh. Where do you work?' Loo asked.

'Uh . . . The name escapes me for the moment . . .' Mr Dumbness stammered. 'The Department of . . . Something . . . What do you take in your tea? Sugar? Lemon? Knock-out drops?'

Whatever was in the tea, it hit the spot – after missing breakfast, Loo didn't even notice the slight chemical flavor, or that the cakes seemed to have small black capsules sticking out of them. Mr Dumbness didn't seem to be eating, only sitting back in his chair, cloven hooves together, cackling quietly to himself. Loo didn't care; more for her.

As Loo gorged, Mr Dumbness told wonderful tales of life in Blarnia. He told of the midnight revels when

the dryads, druids, and droids emerged to play badmin-
ton with a live hand grenade. He told of the White Stag
who gave you wishes if you caught him. He told of how
the Stag was getting old now and really not making
much of an effort to get away. He told of how the Stag
had thus been caught by everyone in Blarnia, including
a paraplegic, and how the Stag never specified that you
couldn't use one of your wishes to wish for more
wishes. So everyone in Blarnia had an infinite number
of wishes, and any time you used one of them, somebody you knew would use one of theirs to reverse it,
just out of spite. Everything was just as dreary and
awful as it had been before the Stag had showed up,
except everyone blamed each other for it, and so the
land was filled with a terrible resentment. 'It's like
living in a damn O. Henry story,' sighed Mr Dumbness. 'Daughter of Steve, how are the crumpets?'

'Mmmfph-mmphff,' Loo said, shoving two more
down her gullet.

'They never fail. I got the recipe from The Marilyn
Monroe Cookbook.' Mr Dumbness was telling her all
about Bacchus' last visit to Blarnia, when everybody
got fanatically pissed and ended up wearing traffic
cones on their heads when he suddenly stopped, as if
remembering the purpose of Loo's visit. 'How are you
feeling?' Mr Dumbness asked. 'Groggy, perhaps?'

'No,' Loo said, mopping up the last smear of raspberry jam with a scrap of crumpet. She popped it into her mouth, then belched loudly.

Wiping his cheek, Mr Dumbness frowned – then his expression relaxed again. 'I think what we need now,' he said, 'is some music.' He went over to the DVD player. 'It plays CDs, too,' he said, fiddling with it. 'Have to wait a bit, for the boiler to get going.'

Thirty minutes later, the most amazing music echoed through the cosy cave. It was unlike anything Loo had ever heard. 'By your expression I take it you're unfamiliar with the work of Jethro Tull,' Mr Dumbness said. 'I find most rock to be so . . . arid, intellectually speaking. But this – listen to that flute!' Mr Dumbness sang along. 'Sitting on a park bench – eyeing little girls with bad intennnt! Hey, Aqualung!'

Loo didn't know what to say to this, so she just sat there smiling, trying to ignore the sudden rumblings in her stomach. Mr Dumbness appeared to be waiting for her to do something, but Loo didn't know what it was.

'Amazing . . . the glassy eyes must be her normal expression,' he said, half to himself. 'Time to take out the big guns.' The Faun pulled a funny little flute made of straw out of his pocket and began to play along. The tune made Loo want to cry and laugh and scream and throw up, all at the same time, but mostly throw up. For the first time, she wondered if this cave had been built with a water-closet.

'Anything?' The girl's innards must be made of cast-iron, the Faun thought to himself. Capering and sweating, Mr Dumbness began doing his best Ian Anderson impression. This never failed to induce coma at parties – if this didn't work, he didn't know what . . .

It wasn't working.

Suddenly Mr Dumbness started to bawl. His big brown eyes filled with tears, and his even bigger pink sinuses with snot, and it all came out like someone had pushed the 'eject' button on his face. The Faun gushed like a hairy little broken faucet, and soon his goatee was soaked with tears and mucus. It was most unattractive.

'Oh, Mr Dumbness!' Loo said. 'Please do get a hold on yourself. I'm already feeling rather ill.'

Mr Dumbness stopped crying, as if a spigot had been turned. 'Really?' he said, voice filled with hope. 'Would you call yourself pre-comatose?'

'No,' Loo said, not knowing what the word meant.

The sobbing began again. 'Oh, I'm a bad faun,' Mr Dumbness blubbered. 'Look at me, Daughter of Steve—'

'I'm trying not to,' Loo mumbled. 'Please don't turn arou— oh God . . .'

'Would you believe I'm the sort of Faun who'd meet

an innocent girl in the woods, pretend to be its friend, and invite it back to my home just so I could give it drugged comestibles and hand it over to the Wide Witch?'

'No,' said Loo firmly. 'You wouldn't do that. You'd *never* do that.'

'But I have.'

'Oh, Mr Dumbness, do stop talking nonsense!' Loo laughed. 'I'm a fairly good judge of people, I think, and—'

'What an imbecile,' Mr Dumbness said into his handkerchief, as he blew his nose loudly. 'I'm doing it right now. I'm kidnapping you.'

Confused, Loo looked behind her. 'Who are you talking to?' she asked.

'I'm talking to *you*, Loo,' said Mr Dumbness. Loo looked behind her again. 'You mean there's someone standing behind me with the same name as me? What are the odds?'

'No! There's only you and me,' said Mr Dumbness, pointing to each party in the small cave. 'We're the only ones here.'

'How odd,' said Loo. 'I must have dematerialized so Mr Dumbness thinks I'm gone. Meanwhile, there's someone else here named Loo – maybe she's an invisi-bomber!' Loo began looking under the cushions for her

invisible German doppelganger. 'Come out, you rotter!
I want to go home to London!' She pulled down a
bookcase.

'Stop – what are you doing to my home? Stop it!'

Loo had taken her butterknife and was cutting a hole
in Mr Dumbness' couch. With a cry, Mr Dumbness
threw himself at her. Grabbing her, he yelled, 'Loo, you
haven't dematerialized! *You're* the one I'm kidnapping.'

There was a long pause. 'Don't get it,' said Loo.

'Listen – you must listen, or else this book will never
get underway,' Mr Dumbness said. 'I've taken service
under the Wide Witch.'

'Who's the —'

'Shut up! I was just getting to that. God, you are
annoying,' Mr Dumbness said. 'The Wide Witch is an
evil sorceress who has taken over Blarnia, and made it
winter all the time. I'd hate summer too, if I weighed
as much as she does.' Loo opened her mouth to speak,
but Mr Dumbness rambled on. 'She told me that if I
ever met a Son of Atom or Daughter of Steve, I was to
abduct them – kidnap them – catch them – and hand
them over to her.'

'I don't see what this has to do with me,' Loo said.
Her stomach was really rumbling now. It was embarrassing, but she had to ask. 'Do you have a potty?'

Mr Dumbness suddenly knew what was about to

happen, and he wanted Loo to be as far away from his belongings as possible when it did. 'Come on, let's go,' he said, pulling her by the arm. 'You're not going to befoul my cave.'

Loo almost made it; the first arrivals spattered Mr Dumbness' welcome mat. She stumbled out of the small opening, and noisily retched. As she emptied the contents of her stomach – quite capacious for an eight-year-old, Mr Dumbness thought grimly – the Faun demanded Loo give him her handkerchief. 'I'm not ruining a piece of my good Irish linen for you,' he said, taking the proffered square and scrubbing at the mat. As he worked and Loo heaved out the barbituate-loaded baked goods, Mr Dumbness recited all the things that the Wide Witch would do to him, if he let Loo go. 'She'll give me a Dutch rub, then an Indian burn, a wedgie – have you ever had one of her wedgies? They're brutal. It's two weeks of salve on the taint, if you're lucky!' Loo seemed to have finished building her gastrointestinal ziggurat in the snow. 'Come back inside,' Mr Dumbness said.

'But Mr Dumbness,' Loo pleaded. 'You can't! You mustn't—'

Mr Dumbness was amazed – did this lame-brain actually, finally understand?

'—I'm not finished,' the girl said, then added a new level to the steaming pile.

'Sod this!' Mr Dumbness said. 'It's not bloody worth it!' Grabbing Loo by the arm again, they began to march towards the traffic light. 'Let her make me into a curry! I'm walking you back to the traffic light, then you can go back to your closet or chest of drawers or wherever the hell you came from.'

'Wardrobe,' Loo said, then threw up again. Mr Dumbness had to leap to avoid the blowback.

'We must move as quickly as we can. Her spies are everywhere . . .' Mr Dumbness said, looking around. 'All they'll have to do is follow the sick . . . I'm sure to get the tickle-torture . . . a nostril-ripper . . .'

'Oh, Mr Dumbness, I think you're being paranoid,' Loo said. 'Who would ever want to give you a nostril-ripper?'

'Bleeding hell!' Mr Dumbness exploded, as they reached the traffic light. 'Do you understand bloody English? Do me a favour – go home and never come back!'

The traffic light was red, so Loo stood at it for a bit. Then, when it turned green, she walked back to the wardrobe. 'What a nice time,' she thought. 'I think Mr Dumbness and I will be great friends!'

CHAPTER 3

When Loo burst from the wardrobe, her siblings were crouched on the floor, ears pressed to the door to the hallway.

'I'm back! I've come ba—' Pete clapped a brawny hand over her mouth.

'Shh!' Sue said, finger to her lips. 'We're hiding from the Professor – he's trying to force us to take hormones.'

They all listened as the Professor and Mrs MacBeth went from door to door, calling out sweetly, then swearing under their breath. 'Hello? Children? I remind you that you are legally obliged to cooperate . . . grubby little bastards . . . devious sons-of-Children, you want to help Science, don't you?'

'Why?' Pete whispered bitterly. 'What's Science ever done for me?'

'How about "allow you to walk among humans as a near-equal"?' Ed countered.

'Listen to me,' Loo said breathlessly. 'I know how we can escape!'

'Does it involve a pommel horse?' Pete whispered.

Not only was his a one-track mind, the track wasn't very wide, either. He tapped on the room's wooden floor fruitlessly. 'If only we could dig a hole somehow.'

'No no! Not that way,' Loo said. 'We can go through the wardrobe!'

'Ri-iight,' Ed whispered. 'Does anybody have Loo's pills?' Loo slugged him ineffectually.

'Where have you been, Loo?' Sue scolded.

'Wherever it was, you got puke in your hair,' snickered Ed. He was sort of rooting for the Professor. Weirdo drugs might make his siblings interesting for once, and there was always the possibility of caging them and charging strangers admission.

'Children, I've got some nice suppositories for you . . .' Mrs MacBeth sang. The Perversies' bottoms clenched with fear.

'It's a magical place!' Loo burbled. 'A whole new world!'

'Uh-huh . . .' Sue remembered the last time Loo discovered 'a whole new world' – inside an old refrigerator at the local dump. Some firemen had to come and cut her out.[5]

'That's nothing,' Ed whispered. 'This morning I

---

[5] Ed's idea to blow the door off with some fireworks hadn't worked. It only made the fridge really hot.

found a passage to Saturn in my bellybutton. And there's a whole alternate reality stuck up my nose.' Ed knew better than to tease Loo, who was unstable under the best of circumstances, but he couldn't help himself.

'Listen, you rotters, it's *real*!' Loo yelled.

The other children knew Loo believed what she was saying with all her heart, but that didn't make it any more likely. Fairies, leprechauns, commercials, she believed in them all. Loo could never be trusted with radios because she knew they were filled with tiny people trapped inside. More times than her siblings could count, they had come upon her sitting with a hammer, sifting through the wreckage, 'looking for survivors.'

But any questions of their sister's sanity had to be tabled for the moment, in light of the more immediate problem caused by Loo's outburst. 'They're in there,' Mrs MacBeth called. 'I heard them.' The hall was filled with the sound of footsteps.

'Little children,' the Professor hollered as he ran, 'the first one who gives themselves up gets to be in the Control group.'

'There's a snowy wood, and a traffic light, and a lovely little man who's really a goat . . .'

'Whatever she's taking now,' Ed confided to Sue, 'we should halve it.'

'Bugger this!' Pete said. 'I'm not going to simply wait here to be caught!'

Pathologically risk-averse, Sue grabbed her brother's arm. 'Pete, don't—'

'This is it! I'm going over the top!' Throwing open the door, he yelled, 'Come and get me, you blighters!' and scurried out into the hallway. Unsure what to do, Sue ran after him.

'There's two of 'em!' the Professor called to Mrs MacBeth. 'Remember — testosterone for the girls, estrogen for the boys!'

Screw that, Ed thought, slamming the door. He'd wait it out; maybe two guinea pigs would be enough for now. 'Loo, don't even think about—' He saw Loo disappearing into the wardrobe. 'Oh, what the . . .'

She'd have to survive on her own. Jamming a chair under the doorknob, Ed moved to the window and opened it. Perfect – there was a skip filled with rubbish directly below. The refuse would cushion his fall, and he could hide in it until nightfall. Then, he could creep down to the river, where the dogs would lose his scent . . .

Ed suddenly heard a voice in his head. It was the author. 'NO,' the voice said. 'GO INTO THE WARDROBE.'

'Are you there, God?' Ed said. 'It's me, Hitler.'

'QUIT REFERENCING OTHER PAROD-IES,' the voice said, 'AND GET INTO THE WARDROBE. THE PUBLISHER WANTS THIS MESS TO BE UNDER 175 PAGES, SO EVERYBODY CAN MAKE AS MUCH MONEY AS POSSIBLE.'

Well, that seemed a little shabby, even to someone who appreciated a quick buck as much as Ed did.[6] 'Okay,' the boy said, flicking a dead bluebottle off the sill in quiet protest.

Outside, the Professor tried the doorknob. 'Come on out! We're not going to hurt you . . . scrotty little blighters . . .' It sounded like he'd been drinking.

Further away, Ed heard Pete yell, 'Hands off my bum!'

Ed knew he was running out of time. He looked around. There wasn't anything in this room but the wardrobe.

'WHAT ARE YOU WAITING FOR?' the voice said. 'I'M GETTING TIRED OF TYPING IN ALL-CAPS.'

---

[6] And Ed surely did. He was the kind of child that roamed the neighbourhood, collecting aluminium cans to sell for scrap. He was determined to have an offshore bank account. Ed hoped you didn't need an actual ocean for one of those; he and a school pal had simply been chucking the money into a local pond.

'Okay, okay,' Ed said, and slipped inside the wardrobe. He'd always planned to do it, he just resented being ordered around. Sweating slightly, breathing in the scent of patchouli and mothballs, Ed stood among the outfits, feeling the satin rubbing up against his face. Through the crack, he saw the Professor open the door quickly, and jab a syringe at roughly buttock-height. When he felt nothing but air, he stepped into the room.

'Damn!' the Professor said. 'Where have those little sods got to?'

The Professor began walking around the room, taking a few steps then whirling about suddenly. 'Ah-HA!' he said, over and over. 'Ah-HA! . . . Oh, I'm dizzy . . .'

To his very great horror, Ed realised that a sneeze was gathering in his sinuses – patchouli always had that effect. The only thing for it was to move back as far as he could, and muffle the sound with a peasant blouse or Nehru jacket or something. As quietly as possible, Ed pulled the wardrobe door shut.

Out of the corner of his eye, the Professor saw the wardrobe door close. 'Who did that?' he barked.

'Only the wind,' came Ed's muffled voice. 'Whooo-ooo.'

'Impossible. The window's shut.'

Ed paused. 'The house is settling,' he said.

'Oh. All right.' The Professor turned to go, then

something clicked. 'Hey, wait—' He rushed over to the wardrobe and wrenched the door open. 'Come out of there, you! Come and let me give you a nice healthy pair of funbags!'

'Funbags? Never!' Hitting the Professor across the face with some love beads, Ed turned and lunged towards the back, hands parting the clothes.

The Professor tried to follow, but fortunately for Ed (and the plot), the shady medico could not overcome his powerful fear of confined spaces. He would screw up his courage, take the tiniest step into the wardrobe – then draw his foot back quickly with a small cry. It was not clear what he thought was sure to take place if he *did* leap inside, but then again, phobias are like that. There was much sweating and stammered curses; finally he bellowed, 'You'll have to come out sometime, you little welsher! And when you do, your suppository will be the biggest, squarest one I can find!'

Ed gulped. Where the blazes was Loo? She had be in here somewhere.

As if on cue, Ed felt something with his foot. Expecting something soft and annoying like a little sister, he kicked it. He was surprised to find it smooth and hard. Ed reached down to massage his hurt toe . . . and found a glass jug, which seemed to have spilled its contents all over the floor of the wardrobe. Maybe it's beer! Ed thought. He put his finger in the puddle, then licked it. It didn't smell like Dad's breath, dash it all. He had no idea what it was; it didn't taste like anything. Maybe he could still say it was beer, and sell it to Pete; Pete's reading ability was pretty shaky.

Wiping his finger on a Peter Max-designed topless bathing suit, Ed noticed that the wardrobe had begun to pulse and sing, but somehow this didn't strike him as being the least bit odd. After a few steps, he found himself in a snowy wood, just as Loo had predicted. This was the only time in Ed's memory that his sister's perceptions had even remotely jibed with reality, and it shocked the older boy to his core. As he walked to the traffic light winking in the middle of the forest, he found himself addressing the possibility that there really *were* little men inside the radio.

Ed felt distinctly odd. Things that he wouldn't have given a second thought to on a normal day, things like sticks and leaves and such, were striking him as incredibly groovy. As he crunched his way through the snow, Ed felt a oneness with all Creation – even with the pile of reindeer droppings directly to his left. Shockingly, it seemed to feel the same way. As he passed, a large link of poo suddenly reared up on its end and gave him a cheery 'Hello!'

'Hello,' Ed said, but didn't stop to talk. He had to

find . . . somebody . . . Who was it, again? If he'd only remembered to speak it into his index finger . . . Then, without warning, Ed entered a new, even groovier level of heaviness, and all his motivation seemed to drain out of the soles of his feet. Ed felt the cold, and wished he had something to eat; he decided to lean up against the traffic light that stood there, winking moronically in the middle of the forest, and see if something edible sauntered by. A squirrel scampered past, whistling ineptly, but no matter how loud he yelled Ed couldn't convince it to get into his mouth. Maybe it didn't understand English.[7]

'It all seems so meaningless,' Ed said to himself, depressed. 'Everybody playing programmed roles, locked inside their arbitrary cultural games . . .' Why look for Loo? Why escape from the Professor? Why do anything? As he leaned there on the traffic light, Ed's brain supplied the only answer; his mind turned towards vague thoughts of girls, something it had been doing more and more lately.

---

[7] The presence of clearly Earthly animals in Blarnia suggests that, as with the land-bridge that once connected Asia to North America, animals crossed from one world to the other via some ancient piece of furniture, sometime in the far distant past. It is generally agreed that the most irritating Earth species started out native to Blarnia, and no wonder.

Ed had learned the rudiments of sex at eight, while at a sleepaway camp for sceptical children. (Though his parents didn't send him there any more – since they had got religion, doing so would be unthinkable – Ed still got the camp's alumni newsletter, 'Prove It'.) One afternoon, Ed and his friends had come upon two dogs hooked together in the middle of the road. They asked a counsellor about it, and her matter-of-fact answer was so alarming – especially in its particulars – that Ed and his pals became outraged and immediately marched straight to Dr Fornuftig, the Danish social scientist who was in charge of the camp. Imagine their surprise when they were told that what the counsellor had said was *true*, right down to the last absurd, awkward detail! In hopes of reassuring them a bit, the scientist showed them lots of diagrams and charts, including one particularly worrying scattergraph. In the years since, Ed's attitude had hardened into a mixture of confusion, secret longing, and apprehension, as well as a tendency to get giggly when certain formerly innocuous phrases were used in conversation.

Although he was determined to be precocious in every other area – even spending an extra year in utero, so as to 'get the jump' on his future classmates – Ed was more than content to let this area of human existence lay dormant for as long as it liked. But more and more his body seemed to have ideas of its own. This was alarming to say the least, and Ed hoped that nothing too embarrassing would happen when the dam finally burst, as he sensed it must. If he made a fool of himself somehow, Ed thought, better it be here, where he didn't know anybody. Whatever happens, it mustn't get back to anybody at school. Ed didn't want to end up like that boy in his form that farted by mistake during an exam; three years later, he was still living it down. As I'm sure I don't need to tell you, ten-year-olds have long memories for such things.[8]

The phrase 'doing it' suddenly popped into Ed's head, and he burst out laughing. Blushing furiously, he looked around the snowy landscape, making sure he was alone.

To Ed's horror, he discovered that he wasn't – far off in the distance, Ed could see a large sledge coming his way. He steeled himself, hoping that he wouldn't think of 'doing it' again and laugh. Unfortunately, the effort of not thinking of 'doing it,' insured that he thought of 'doing it,' and giggled like a madman.

---

[8] If we count Ed's extra year in the womb, he was nearly eleven. But since Mrs Perversie considered everything related to reproduction to be miraculous and highly embarrassing, I will not mention it again.

Even though it was still some distance off, Ed could see that the vehicle was pulled by at least twenty reindeer, all good-sized and dressed in black leather. Their bells tinkled a cheery tune as they approached, one that Ed eventually identified as 'Sympathy for the Devil.'

Despite the fact that so many powerful creatures were pulling with all their might, the sledge moved very slowly. As the contraption drew closer, Ed discovered why: while the driver appeared to be smaller, about the size of a dormitory refrigerator, the passenger was massively obese, bigger by far than any person Ed had ever seen.

'Hurry up!' Ed heard the passenger yell. 'I want to make this light.'

The small, lumpy man cracked his whip, and the reindeers strained hard. Some actually shat with the effort, and yet the sledge continued to crawl. Its runners dug into the snow, grinding up the wet dirt below. The dwarf driver whipped some more, then got out and feverishly exhorted the reindeer like the crowd at the frenzied finish line of a marathon. Presently, the sledge crept to the light, which had turned red. Disheartened, the driver clambered back to his place.

'Damn,' the large passenger said. Ed now saw her in detail, a thirty-stone specimen with skin as white as a teetotaller's conscience. Half enchantress, half manatee, she had cruel red lips, a pug-like mien, and a crown with sharp points upon which emergency baked potatoes were speared. She seemed to grow fatter right before one's eyes, and yet her clothes still held; this was the awesome dark magic harnessed by the Wide Witch. While she had the outward form of a human, such a creature couldn't be human. Too evil for just one gender, she wasn't truly female, either. And she definitely wasn't English.

Sitting at the light, spilling out of the sledge like a rubbish bag filled with salad cream, the Witch fidgeted. She examined her latest batch of press-on nails, which spelled out IM PURE EVIL – or had, before they started chipping. 'I simply *must* torture my manicurist.'

The Wide Witch took a savage chomp from a defenceless chocolate bar. The light changed, but the sledge didn't move. 'Come on!' The woman dealt the driver a smack that made his eyes bug out. (She was a hit-first-and-ask-questions-later type boss.) 'Why aren't we moving?' she demanded. 'I'm *starving* back here.'

'We're stuck,' the dwarf said.

'Well, whip them more! Do it like you mean it!'

'Yes, ma'am,' the dwarf said, pretending to do so. He was opposed to violence, but jobs were quite hard to come by in Blarnia.[9] So his solution had been to teach the reindeer to dodge his whip, which they did quite nimbly.

'I don't know why they act like that,' the woman grumbled at the sight of her team ducking and jittering this way and that. 'It looks like they're having a fit. Other reindeer don't have fits.'

'I told you,' the dwarf said over his shoulder, 'these is special reindeer. They're eee-vil, Your Majesty, like you are.'

'If they're so special why aren't we moving?'

'Because you're a bleedin' ruminant, that's why!' the dwarf longed to shout, but he knew that was more than his hide was worth. He'd seen his boss eat things bigger than he was, without even chewing. So he kept his mouth shut, and whipped some more.

I suppose you'll be wanting to know why this woman was – I'm searching for the proper expression – globally rotund. No, 'rotund' isn't quite right – that suggests roundness, fullness, a pleasingly abundant quality, and there was nothing pleasant about the

---

[9] Most Blarnian companies had moved to Wonderland, which had tremendous tax advantages. Those that had stayed outsourced all the jobs to Middle Earth, where you could pay people simply by not killing them. In Middle Earth, 'not-getting-killed an hour' was a damn fine wage.

Queen. This woman was more like a dollop. And it had nothing to do with enjoying her food, I can tell you that. Food was just a means to an end, the end being becoming as huge as possible.

Like many rulers, the Queen (who was also called the Wide Witch, for obvious reasons) was interested in constantly expanding her territory. And while there were certain things she could control in the outside world – the weather, for example, which she kept eternally Winter, so that she might sweat less – this was a distant second to actually enlarging her real domain, her physical body. Her doctor had told her that this was an unwise policy, but then she solved that problem by eating him on the spot. She was fierce, and terrible, and a definite weirdo.

Ed was content to stand there passively, and watch the scene unfold. He was busy devolving. Thanks to the psychedelic banana-peel extract he'd unwittingly dosed himself with back in the Professor's Swinging Sixties wardrobe, young Ed Perversie became convinced he could reverse evolution on a cellular level, using only his mind. He was hoping to make it all the way back before it got dark. At the moment, however, he was stuck at paramecium.

The dwarf stopped whipping, and heaved himself out of the sledge. 'Got to butter the runners,' he said, producing a pack from his pocket. He kept it there for just one-tenth of a second too long.

'Thank God!' The woman swiped the butter in one fluid motion; she could move surprisingly fast, when food was involved. There was no time to take off the foil – she simply squeezed it hard, and the contents shot into her mouth. 'I was about to pass out,' she said, licking her fingers. Then the light changed from green to red again, and a fresh roar of frustration issued from the titanic female. She poked the dwarf savagely with her long, golden fork; she carried it at all times, so that she might spear anything edible that the sledge cruised by.

'Get back here and whip those reindeer!' It was so hard to get good help, especially if you were evil and offered only three paid holidays per annum, anti-Christmas, anti-Easter, and a 'floater' representing sneering antipathy to all other world religions. They made a strange picture; the woman poking the dwarf, the dwarf whipping the reindeer. Eventually her arm got tired and she stopped. She found a bag of crisps in the folds under her armpit, and dumped them into her maw.

'What's wrong with you?' she asked the dwarf. 'Don't you feel me poking you?'

'Oh yes, Your Majesty,' the dwarf replied.

'Well, doesn't it hurt?' the Queen demanded.

'Very much, Your Majesty, I can hardly stand it,' the dwarf lied. 'It's *excruciating*.' (He had, in fact, slipped a baking tray under his jerkin.)

'I command you to scream a little this time. I need the encouragement.' As she prepared to begin another round of pokery, she noticed Ed, leaning against the traffic light. 'Who the hell are you?' she said, lightly spraying crisp crumbs.

'My name is Ed,' Ed said, in his paramecium voice.

'Do you have any food?'

'No.' Ed raised his finger and spoke into it. 'Question: what do parameciums eat?'

'I haven't a clue,' the Queen said haughtily, thinking the boy was speaking to her, 'but I know what *I* eat, and if you value your life you had better start pushing!'

CHAPTER 4

 After a Herculean effort, two herniated rein-deer, and a lot of swearing on Ed's part, the sledge had moved a grand total of sixteen inches.

'You could get out, you know,' Ed said.

'I don't see how that would change anything,' the Queen said, examining her knuckles. You could still see them. They simply weren't fat enough.

'Memo to self,' Ed spoke into his finger. 'This sucks.'

'You should be proud and grateful to help your Queen,' the woman said.

'Queen?' Ed said, already longing for his good old paramecium days. 'Tcha, right. Queen of the buffet, maybe.'

'Silence, whelp! I am Queen of all that you see—' she swept her arm wide '—all Blarnia!'

Ed's cupidity, never far from the surface, awoke with a start. 'So I suppose you're loaded?'

'I don't know what you mean.'

Bingo! Ed thought. 'I'm through pushing,' Ed

announced, then turned to the dwarf. 'Move over, de Sade.'

The dwarf, a humanitarian (or reindeeritarian, at least) was cut to the quick. 'It's not what you think,' he whispered, but Ed didn't hear.

Ed slid into the sledge opposite the Queen. 'Blarnia? Is that what this dump is called?' Ed was trying to be hard-boiled, because he was more than a little intimidated by attractive women. And while the woman in the sledge might not be everybody's cup of suet, she certainly was Ed's. Now here was a woman you could lose yourself in – and rich, besides! Only really rich people denied it, Ed thought. Had the boy done a little more research in his father's top drawer he might've discovered he came from a long line of 'chubby chasers,' admirers of the plus-sized gal. For generations, male Perversies had come out of Puberty's crucible, eager to bury themselves in generous folds of sagging love. He leaned over and put his hand on the Queen's knee. 'If I said you had a beautiful body . . .'

'. . . I'd say you were lying,' the Queen said, swallowing a cupcake whole. For all her power, she really felt quite crummy about herself; low self-esteem was the original source of her wickedness. Desperate for friends, she had joined the Evil-ness Club at her school, and things had snowballed from there.

Her self-loathing showed in the condition of her sledge, too: the vehicle was full of sticky detritus – chocolate wrappers, sat-upon chips, and toddler-sized drink cups leaking fizzless fizzy drinks. As he pried his feet from the floor, Ed looked at the Queen more closely. In her white furs, and with her even whiter skin, she resembled nothing so much as a crowned dollop of mashed potatoes. Ed started counting her chins, but stopped after he hit double-digits. Ed had been waiting for a woman like this his entire life, and every time he looked at her, his barely born libido crowed like an electric rooster. It was in that moment – when he became unable to form sentences in the presence of a female he found attractive, that poor Ed became a man.

I should perhaps keep my distance from her mouth, Ed thought. I'll hop back down to the — BRAAAAAAA! The poor boy's synapses fired, the rooster brayed, and it was all he could do not to drool openly.

The Queen poked him with her golden fork. 'What's your problem?'

'Durr . . .' Ed said. What was he supposed to do? He plucked something out of the air, pretending to be the male lead in one of the soap operas Sue watched so incessantly. 'Relax, baby. I'm a man, you're a woman . . .'

'Woman?' the Queen snorted. 'You must be joking.'

Ed did the maths, and whipped his hand away.

Something seemed to occur to the Queen. 'Wait – did you say you were a *man*?'

Ed blushed. 'Well, okay, I'm only ten.' That sounded awful, Ed thought, so he added. 'Nearly eleven – and I'm mature for my age.' Were seven body hairs a lot or a little? Ed decided not to mention it.

'A Son of Atom,' the Queen mused. 'I've never met one of those. You're much bigger than I thought you'd be . . .'

Ed flexed his scrawny muscles, trying to work it.

'. . . just perfect for lunch . . .' The woman removed a napkin tucked in her sleeve and tied it around her neck. Then she extracted a pepper-grinder from a hidden cupboard, and ground it over Ed's head.

I think she's into me, Ed thought silently. Trying not to seize up in anticipation for what was certainly about to happen, he tried to make conversation. 'You know, it's the funniest thing, I got here via a wardrobe! I was looking for my little brat of a sister – do you have any sisters? How about gold bullion? What are you going to do with that fork?'

Eyes burning, lips smacking, the Queen loomed over Ed, fork raised and ready to tuck in . . . Then she had a thought: What if I develop a taste for it? What if

humans are like Chinese food, and thirty minutes after
I eat this boy I desperately want another? She remembered after the dwarf had introduced her to squirrel
fritters, and now the entire forest was empty. The few
squirrels that survived had taken to disguising themselves as birds. 'Erm – did you say you had a sister? A
Daughter of Steve?'

'Yeah,' Ed said, knowing instinctively that he'd
better change the subject if he wanted to score with
this chick. 'She's a dork. Anyway—'

What if Daughters of Steve taste better than Sons
of Atom? the Queen thought to herself. She couldn't
afford to take the chance – so she set on a new course of
action. The Queen put away her salt shaker and fork.
'Would you like a drink?' she said sweetly. 'A martini,
perhaps?'

Ed had seen enough James Bond movies to know
that this was a great sign. Only high-class babes offered
you a martini. 'Yes, please,' he said. Then, thinking he
might've seemed overeager, he looked at his watch. 'Of
course, I have one every day at this time.'

'Ten-thirty in the morning? My, my.' Sons of Atom
made poor liars, the Queen thought with satisfaction, as
she extracted a silver shaker from a hidey-hole in the
sledge.

'Nice,' Ed said, genuinely impressed.

'Makes the long delays more tolerable,' she said, shooting a dirty look in the dwarf's direction.[10] 'Gin or vodka?'

'Both,' Ed said coolly, trying to show what a Devil-may-care rascal he was.

'O . . . kay,' the Queen said, shaking the shaker, then handing Ed the shiny metal cup.

'Thanks,' Ed said, then he caught a whiff of it – it smelled like cleaning fluid. 'Bottoms up,' he said, trying to keep the smile on his face until the cup hid it from the Queen's view. He drank a tiny bit – it tasted awful. The liquor burned – he could feel all the tissues of his mouth shrinking back from it. His tongue went numb almost instantly; shock, perhaps. At least the olive was edible. He put the cup down, and the Queen saw his face, already flushed.

The Queen had lit up a cigarette, to stave off her appetite. 'I can see you're hungry,' the Queen said, exhaling tobacco smoke in the boy's face. 'Not much left around here, I'm afraid,' she added, rummaging through a score of secret stashes and tossing out mounds of empty packages. 'We were just on our way back home for lunch. Of course, he'—the Queen

[10] One of the reindeer had suffered a heart attack, and he was giving it mouth-to-mouth.

pointed at the dwarf, who had got out some heart paddles and was pressing them against the body of the lifeless reindeer—'eats everything in sight. I think he has an eating disorder.'

'Oh, rather,' Ed nodded conspiratorially. Just agree with everything she says, laugh at all her jokes, and . . . Next stop, her place! Ed wondered if she had anything valuable there that she wouldn't miss.

The Queen was now digging between the seats. 'Ah, the last morsel,' she said, wiping off a small cellophane package. 'Would you like some Turkish Delight?'

'Yes, please!' Ed said. Excellent. That sounds dirty! Unfortunately, his bitterness doubled when he realized that Turkish Delight not only wasn't some exotic sexual practice, but also a misleading trade name for 'crap.' As he chewed the cloying, parching square, Ed felt a great outpouring of sympathy for the entire Turkish people. Suddenly, there didn't seem to be enough saliva in the entire world. 'Do you have any water?' Ed croaked.

'Come on, goddamnit! Hang in there, Lightning!' the dwarf yelled, and applied the paddles again. 'Clear!' The reindeer convulsed.

'Get some snow,' the Queen said. She knew lust when she saw it, and pegged Ed to be the kind of man who could be made to do anything.

Ed leapt from the sledge, as the Queen lit up another

cigarette. 'Would you like to come back to my place?' she asked.

Ed's mouth was packed with slowly melting snow, so he simply nodded frenziedly in the affirmative.

'Well, you can't – I'm not that type of lady. I don't take strangers back to my place. I have to get to know them first. I live alone, you see, and you can never be too careful. We've only just met, I don't even know your name—'

'Ed,' Ed said, trying to climb back aboard.

'No, please, Ed – stay down there. Don't ruin it by going too fast. I like you, Ed, I like you very much—'

Ed blushed at a sudden tightness in his trousers.

'—but I need more time. I'd like to meet your family for one thing.'

The tightness diminished. 'If you mean my parents,' Ed said, 'that's impossible. They sold us.'

'What a terrible pity,' the Queen said, not feeling sorry at all. 'So am I correct in assuming that you wouldn't mind too terribly if something . . . were to happen to them?'

'Oh, God, no,' Ed said. 'Not as long as I could get the will straightened out beforehand.'

'And your siblings . . . ?'

'Even more useless. Actually, Sue's all right – boring,

but not openly psychotic like the other two,' Ed said. 'My brother Pete actually believes that he goes to a public school called Chillblains. He's really just down in the cellar.'

'How many of you are there?' the Queen said.

'Four,' Ed said.

'That's not very many!' the Queen said, suddenly angry. 'Hardly a mouthful! How many Sons of Atom and Daughters of Steve are there, in total, on the other side of this looking-glass?'

'Wardrobe,' Ed corrected. What was it about fantasy authors and decor? Ed thought for a second, trying to remember the fact he'd learned in school but just as promptly forgotten. 'About four billion,' he said, 'but don't hold me to that – I didn't do very well on that exam.'

The Queen's eyes lit up. 'Four billion! Think about it! If we could convince some of them to holiday here, I could eat as many as I wanted, and we'd still get more tourist money than bloody Middle Earth . . .' The Wide Witch had been doing a slow burn ever since Middle Earth had come out with its massively popular tourism campaign, 'Middle Earth: It's Hobbit-Forming!' 'We need a snappy slogan, though,' she said. 'It all starts with the slogan.'

'How about "Blarnia: It Doesn't Suck"?' the dwarf

offered, writing out a prescription for blood-thinners and sticking it under the reindeer's collar.

The Witch considered. 'Hmm. A bald-faced lie. I like that. Bold choice, but these are bold times.' She paused, searching for Ed's name.

'Ed,' Ed supplied.

'That's right, how silly of me,' she said. 'One doesn't forget somebody like you, Ed.'

Ed's thermometer went into the red again.

''Scuse me,' the dwarf said, pushing past Ed into the sledge. The weak-hearted reindeer was back in harness. 'Pull!' the dwarf yelled, cracking the whip well above the reindeer's heads.

Amazingly, the sledge began to move. Well, creep really; the packets and wrappers that the Queen had tossed out during her search for food had diminished the weight just enough.

'Ed, go back through the wardrobe and get your siblings,' the Queen said. The sledge was moving so slowly that Ed barely had to take a step.

'But why?' Ed said. 'They're arseholes.'

'What a charming, erm, man you are,' the Queen said. 'Will you do that for me? Bring them here?'

'Okay,' Ed said, not at all pleased.

'Good,' the Queen said. 'Then, after I meet them, you and I can be alone.' She remembered something, and reached into her wrappings. 'Here, have them bathe in this before hand,' the Queen said, handing the scrap to Ed, who was still barely three feet away. 'It's a marinade.'

'Okay,' Ed said.

'Then, *au revoir, mon petit entrée du futur,*' the Queen said, blew a kiss, and turned around.

French! The language of love! 'Goodbye!' Ed waved for a long time; it took them an hour to get out of sight.

The sledge was about the size of a five pence piece and Ed was still vaguely tumescent, when he heard Loo's voice, coming from the woods behind him.

'Ohhh, wowww . . .' Loo was stumbling through the snow, tripping occasionally over chunks of air. She was looking at her hand. 'I've never really looked at my hand before,' Loo said. 'Isn't it wonderful?'

'Where the hell did you get off to?' Ed snapped. Sexual frustration can do that to a boy.

'With Mr Dumbness . . . listening to Seventies prog-rock,' Loo said.

'That's your goat friend?' Ed said.

'He's a Faun, only not like a normal Faun. He's divided vertically,' Loo said. 'Front-to-back. It's a birth effect.'

'Defect, you mean.' His sister Loo, associating with strangers? Listening to Seventies progressive rock?

Clearly he hadn't been the only one changed by that wardrobe. As if to second the point, Loo burst into song.

' "Snot is running down his nose!" ' she sang. ' "Greasy fingers smearing shabby clothes! Hey, Aqua-lung!" '

For the millionth time, Ed had the thought that being around insane people was really quite boring. It's like how it is with drunks, only fun if you're drunk, too.

'We've been telling unkind jokes. Would you like to hear one?' Loo giggled. 'It's about the Wide Witch. She calls herself the "Queen" but really she's not. She's so mean and fat, a big fat meany is what . . .'

'Have you ever met her?' Ed said, taking offence. A certain type of boy considers disagreement on matters of attractiveness as a personal insult. 'Maybe she has a glandular problem.'

'Oh, no, not her,' Loo said, hardly able to contain herself. 'She's just *heinous* . . .'

'Who says? Have you ever met her? Have you?'

'No,' Loo admitted. 'Why are you freaking out, dude?'

Dude? 'Perhaps some people find her quite hot,' Ed sniffed. 'Come on, let's go back and get the others . . . Hanging out with bloody goats,' Ed shot out of the side of his mouth. 'Pete'll thump me for letting you do that. Tell me, did you two eat a tin can?'

Loo blushed. 'No,' she said a bit too quickly. Mr Dumbness had eaten a tablecloth. 'You don't look very well,' she said, changing the subject.

'I'm fine.' Oh no! Ed thought, sure that his inappropriate lust was written all over his face.

'No you're not. You look flushed.'

'I— I—' Ed stammered. He would have to do better once he was around the others. How could he ever hide his secret shame, his ferocious love of plus-sized girls? 'I'm just cold,' Ed said, kicking a squirrel dressed as a bird.

'Look, everybody! I'm really *flying*!' the squirrel squeaked, just before it bounced off a tree.

CHAPTER 5

 When the pair emerged from the wardrobe, it took them a while to find Pete and Sue. Both of the older children lay in cots in a remote storage room, sleeping heavily. It was obvious why: each bore the mark of the Professor's fiendish experiments. Thanks to a mega-dose of hormones, sizeable breasts swelled under Pete's shirt, and Sue had a long, square-ended, Biblical-style beard.

As you can imagine, Ed and Sue sat and laughed at their siblings for a long time. Finally Ed tried to wake Pete up by slapping him, but that was useless. So he kept slapping his brother just for its profound psychological benefits.[11]

'Here,' he said to Loo. 'Free shots.'

Loo gave her older brother a slap across the jaw, then dived under the bed, expecting Pete to roar to life, burning with vengeance. After he didn't, Loo proceeded to get really into it, peppering Pete's motionless body with swats.

[11] To Ed, obviously.

'This is *brilliant*,' Loo said, cheeks flushed and eyes shining.

'It's really good for stress,' Ed said, joining in.

Eventually Peter awoke, spoiling their fun. 'God, I feel like absolute crap,' Pete said, sitting up. 'Like I've been beaten up.'

Ed didn't say a word, he just pointed at Pete's sternum.

Pete looked down the collar of his shirt and screamed.

That woke Sue up. She rubbed the sleep out of her eyes, then felt her beard. 'Ahhh!' she yelled. The pair of them just sat there screaming – Pete's voice higher than before, Sue's much lower – until Ed handed them each a barf bag from the nightstand between the cots.

'Breathe into these,' Ed said. That worked until Pete looked over at Sue, and saw how *she* had changed. Sue did the same and a fresh round began.

Ed sat there until he couldn't stand it any longer, then turned to Loo and shouted, 'Shall we wait outside?'

'Yes!' Loo said, fingers in her ears.

Finally Pete and Sue wore themselves out, and the screaming drifted into self-pity and bickering.

'At least you can shave it off,' Pete griped.

'At least you'll be popular,' Sue spat back.

Ed and Loo came back in and sat down.

'Oh, Pete,' Loo said, 'Ed and I have both been to Blarnia now! It's the best, greatest, most fun—'

'I'm confused,' Sue said. 'Is "been to Blarnia" some sort of new slang?'

Pete rounded on Ed. 'Look here, if you've got Loo mixed up in anything perverted . . .'

Perverted? He knows! He knows! It's written all over my face, Ed thought. 'Uh . . . no,' Ed said.

Pete reached over and grabbed a handful of Ed's shirt. 'I don't believe you!' He was in a foul temper, which was really quite understandable. Few boys Pete's age could go from zero to a C-cup overnight and not be a little off-balance.

'Stop it, you two,' Sue said. 'Let's listen to Loo babble. It's comforting.'

It *was* comforting. '. . . and there's trees, and snow, and a traffic light, and a faun, who's vertical, 'cause he's got a birth effect, with a flute, and lots of classic rock!' Loo said excitedly.

'She just rolls on for hours . . .' Sue said languidly.

'Guys! Guys!' Loo said, desperate for more attention. 'Listen to the song Mr Dumbness taught me.' She cleared her throat and sang, ' "Sitting on a park bench, eyeing little girls with bad intent"—'

Pete didn't need to hear any more. He bolted out of

bed and began chasing Ed around the room. 'I leave you with Loo just once, and this is what happens!' He grabbed Ed and began twisting his arm. 'I should give you a bit of what I gave that guy on my rugby team! I should—'

'—kiss me?' Ed yelled defiantly, dodging behind a bed – but the chase was over almost before it started. Ever the natural athlete, Pete soon had Ed face down on the floor, arms wrenched behind him with a knee in the small of Ed's back.

'I'll teach you to let my little sister get hurt!' Pete said. He had eighteen months of puberty on Ed, and wasn't afraid to use it.

'Wait! It's not my fault!' Ed said, pulling something out of the air. 'Loo didn't protect me, either! *I* was attacked by a giant clam!'

Pete looked puzzled for a moment, then his face screwed up in anger once again. He got up and ran at Loo, who was sitting on the bed, still chatting excitedly to Sue.

'. . . and he lives in a cave, and there's delicious tea, and ACK—'

'Bastard!' Pete said, clamping his rugger-callused mitts around Loo's tender throat. 'I'll teach you to let my little brother get hurt!'

Ed laughed to himself; Pete's impulses towards

~ 71 ~

protecting his siblings would've been admirable, if they weren't so nonsensical and destructive.

Sue let them fight for a bit, then grabbed a glass of water from the table between the beds and dashed it into Pete's face. 'Enough!' she said. 'That does it! First thing tomorrow, we're all going to march directly to the Professor and find out everything there is to know about this wardrobe. Who made it, what type of wood it is – everything!'

Ed blanched; what if the Professor knew about the Wide Witch? 'But Sue,' Ed said, 'what if he thinks we're crackers?'

'I don't care,' Sue said. 'This wardrobe is tearing us apart.'

Now it was Pete's turn. 'Sue,' he said, 'we didn't like each other to begin with.'

Once Sue had made her mind up, there was no shaking her – her imagination simply didn't have enough room to turn around. And so the next morning, more than a little frightened, the children went to see the Professor. Pete, the bravest, knocked on the study door.

'One second,' they heard the Professor say. 'Come in.'

Pete, Sue, Ed and Loo walked into the study. First they noticed all the bizarre and unnerving medical specimens that lay around the room. A gangrenous arm floated in a cloudy preservative; a two-headed baby swam in a cloudy bell-jar. The Professor was behind his desk, speaking into a telephone, playing with a plaster death mask as he talked. He covered the receiver. 'I'll be with you in a moment.' He spoke into the phone. 'Sorry, a new batch of subjects just came in. What were we talking about? Oh, yes – why use children to test drugs and procedures? We just stumbled on it, really; the activists were making it harder and harder to use animals. Fewer people get their knickers in a twist about children . . . No, as long as we pay the parents, they've got no problem with it. Turns out to be much cheaper than monkeys or rabbits, and you don't have to translate the results between species, either. Something that makes a monkey's eyelids peel off might be fine for humans. But if a kid's eyelids flap away – well, then, you can't release that drug. Maybe in the third world, but here the National Institute of Research would scream bloody murder . . . No, thank you. It's my pleasure. Call back if you have any questions.'

The Professor put the phone down. 'Sorry. Interview for *The Times*. A lot of people are very interested in what we're doing here,' he said. 'We're on the forefront of science. Isn't it fun?'

He saw Sue examining a long, rope-like object that ran around the cornice of the room.

'Do you like it?' Professor Berke said. 'Dried tapeworm. Longest one ever captured alive.' As the children gagged, the Professor continued: 'I hope everyone's attitude has improved a bit. Have you come to say you're sorry for how you acted at breakfast yesterday? Pete, have you apologized to Mrs MacBeth for biting her? Not to mention calling her a "grotty old _____ who _____ donkeys." '[12]

Sue saw Pete's eyes flash, and spoke quickly. 'Actually, Professor, we came about something else . . .' As the story poured from Sue, the Professor fiddled with his stethoscope, reading the heartbeats of his desk blotter, the phone, and the bottom of Ed's shoe. When Sue had finished, he slipped the earpieces down on his neck and said something none of them expected.

'Ed,' he said gravely, 'I'm sorry to tell you this, but your shoe is dead.'

'Jesus Christ!' Ed said, disgusted.

'That's not fair! You've been reading ahead!' the other characters said as one.

The Professor continued, 'How do you know Loo's story isn't true? Does Loo usually tell the truth?'

'Ye-es,' Sue said uncertainly. 'Lying means knowing

[12] Thanks, CensorVision!

what's real and what's not, and that's not a strength of Loo's.'

'Fair enough,' Professor Berke said. 'She's truthful. And she's not mad – you can tell that just by looking at her. There are only three possibilities: one, that Loo is lying, but you say she is a truthful person. Two, that she is mad, and we know she isn't, simply by looking at her. Logically, this leaves only one possible outcome . . .'

'That we're on some sort of reality television programme, where people pretend to go to other worlds via pieces of furniture, then try to convince their siblings for cash and prizes!' Sue exclaimed. 'Where are the cameras?'

'Dear oh dear,' the Professor said firmly, 'how ridiculous. What *are* they teaching in schools these days? The only possible outcome, as strange as it may seem, is that your sister Loo is telling the truth.'

'_____!' Ed exploded. 'There's nothing wrong with the schools, the problem is you're as barmy as the rest of this lot! First, people can be mostly truthful and tell lies when it suits them. In fact, the more truthful you usually are, the more likely it is somebody will believe you when you're lying.'

'I don't see what you're getting at,' the Professor said.

'People don't come in two flavours, liars and non-liars, each wearing different-coloured jumpsuits,' Ed said. 'And the idea that you could diagnose insanity just by looking at someone – where did you get your degree from, anyway?'

The Professor cleared his throat. 'That's beside the point,' he said. 'What's important is that Loo here has discovered a new world. Now, the next step is obvious: can we enslave the natives? If not, we'll have to swindle them. Are any of you lawyers?'

'But sir,' Sue said. 'Whenever Loo comes back from—'

'Blarnia,' Loo said.

'—from Blarnia, she's always convinced she's been there for hours, when only a few minutes have passed.'

The Professor looked thoughtful. 'So,' he said, 'if we sold time-shares, you could go on holiday for the rest of your life, and when you got back . . .'

'. . . Your holiday would hardly have started!' Ed chimed in.

'Now, if you had come to me saying, "Loo disappears for hours at a time, and when she comes back, it's hours later', I'd say she was lying. Reality simply doesn't work like that. But this time-shifting business – it's more evidence that Loo is telling the truth.'

Ed smelled money, and was sure the Professor did,

too. In that case, he couldn't appear too excited. 'How do you call that "evidence"?' Ed carped.

The Professor paid no attention. 'Think of it! All that extra space! I can finally put up my model train set!'

Ed got up. 'This is ridiculous,' he said, and stomped towards the door.

'Wait, wait,' the Professor said, rushing over to where Ed stood. Putting his arm around Ed's shoulder, he pointed to a small mirror on the wall. 'Smile, you're on Hidden Camera!'

'I knew it!' Sue said, jumping up and down.

The music started, confetti dropped from the ceiling, and the sound of a studio audience could be heard. This really was the strangest house.

'Come on, Ed, admit it,' the Professor said. 'I got you.'

'Shut up,' Ed said bluntly.

The Professor refused to have his spirits dashed. 'Don't be a spoilsport, come back over here and sit down . . . There's a good chap. I had you all going there, for a bit – you should've seen your faces.'

'But . . . but there really *is* another world,' Loo said, on the verge of tears. 'I've been there, I've seen it! My friends! Mr Dumbness . . . Jethro Tull . . .'

'No, Loo, if that's the wardrobe I think it is, your friends are simply hallucinations caused by a massive dose of a drug popular back in the sixties. Concentrated banana-peel extract. "The Dreaded Yellow Freak-Out." '

'It's not! It's not! It's real! Blarnia's—'

The Professor produced a tranquilliser gun out of his desk and casually shot Loo, who promptly collapsed into a slumber. 'You all don't mind, do you? She looked like she needed some quiet time.'

'No, no,' Sue said. 'Actually, if you have an extra one of those . . .'

'Didn't anybody notice the hippie clothes in there?' the Professor asked. 'Swinging London, man. I got them all at a wild store called "I Was Lord Kitchener's Valet".' He chuckled. 'Crazy times. I should sell that junk on eBuy . . . If you took that banana-peel stuff, I'm surprised you ended up in a place where gravity still worked. I got that batch from a roadie for The Electric Prunes . . . or was it The Strawberry Alarm Clock?'

Ed was puzzled. If Blarnia was just hallucinations, why did Loo and I go to the same place? If the Wide Witch was just a figment of his imagination, he wasn't sure he wanted to believe the Professor. 'Is it safe to go there?' Ed asked, then harrumphed, 'I mean, not that I've ever been.'

Something about the way the Professor looked at him – or the way he mouthed the words 'You're lying' –

told Ed that he knew. 'No, Blarnia's not safe. Don't go in there again – and I'm not just saying that because it might skew my test results. I can't risk any of you doing anything nasty to yourselves and having the Institute coming down on me. As long as I'm leasing you lot, that wardrobe is off limits.' The Professor got up. 'Now, please come with me. It's time for your morning shots. Ed, Loo, you'll be the control group.'

Naturally, once they had been forbidden to return, going back to Blarnia became the all-consuming passion of the Perversie children. Ed still nursed secret hopes of something – perhaps physical, perhaps larcenous – between himself and the Wide Witch. Loo was anxious to pick up the mix tape Mr Dumbness had told her would be waiting. Pete was determined to establish a Crown Colony. Even Sue, normally so pliant in the face of authority, seemed to be in favour of it precisely because the Professor had told them not to. (Ed chalked it up to the testosterone.)

However, as much as they might want to return, getting back to Blarnia wouldn't be easy. The wardrobe had been padlocked, and though Sue thought she could pick it,[13] that would take some time. And whenever

---

[13] Girl Guides again.

they themselves went skulking near that particular room, they always found the Professor skulking there as well.

The next morning after breakfast, Sue, Ed, and Loo gathered in an upstairs room for the now-familiar ritual of comparing symptoms. This room, one of the few without a gas leak in it, had become the children's informal HQ. Ed was pacing about, nervously plotting their next move. 'If we don't make it out soon,' he said, 'Pete will be too busty to fit down any tunnel!'

The two girls crouched in a corner making dust animals. 'Do you think the Professor's telling the truth, Ed?' Sue asked. 'About it just being hallucinations?'

'No, I don't,' Ed said. 'And anyway, even if it is just hallucinations, it's a damn sight more fun than hanging about this bloody house!' He opened a window and threw a book out, just for spite.

Suddenly, Pete burst in. 'On your knees, wog!' Pete bellowed, giving Ed's bottom a prodigious swat with a cricket bat he'd found. 'I hereby claim Blarnia in the name of Her Majesty the Queen!'

'Ow! You _____-_____!' Ed yelled, rubbing his arse. 'You're pretty tough for a bloke with tits!'

'Take that back!' Pete roared, rearing back for a head shot.

Sensing that blood was about to be spilled, Sue leapt

in. 'Would Blarnians technically be "wogs"?' she asked. 'Loo, did your friend look foreign?'

'Ra-*ther*,' Loo said.

'Say, Sue,' Pete said. 'I just had an odd notion. Do you think – do you think we might be in a children's book?'

'Pish-tosh,' Sue said. 'That's ridiculous. Do I look like a character in a children's book?' She scratched herself.

'I see your point,' Pete said. 'But it *would* explain a lot. Why Mum and Dad sold us, for example . . . and all the rot Loo's been talking about other worlds and mythological creatures and whatnot.'

'It is not rot!' Loo yelled.

'Ed,' Sue called to her brother, who was sitting in a corner trying to carve a revolver out of some soap. (The bar was almost gone, so the resultant gun was about the size of a gherkin.) 'Ed, do you think we're all in a children's book?'

Ed didn't look up. ''Course we are. Haven't you noticed the page numbers?' he said, pointing downwards.

Before Sue could respond, the sounds of commotion erupted from downstairs.

'What's that?' Sue asked. The boys shrugged.

Just then the door opened, and Mrs MacBeth stuck

her florid face into the room. 'Make yourselves scarce,' the housekeeper commanded. 'It's a surprise inspection from the National Institute of Research! I told the Professor not to speak to the press! And there's blood everywhere, oh dear, oh dear . . .' She closed the door with a slam.

The sudden draught swept away Loo's menagerie. 'Oh, poo,' she said.

The children shared a look. 'Are you thinking what I'm thinking?' Ed asked.

Without another word, they all ran for the room containing the wardrobe.

CHAPTER 6

 The lock on the wardrobe looked fierce – big and slightly rusty – but it opened with a pliant click. 'Simple,' Sue said merrily, slipping the lock off its hasp. Like many another matron, Sue combined outward respectability with hidden reserves of petty criminality.[14] From the way she was beaming, one would've thought she'd just knocked over a bank, not busted into England's finest collection of ancient hippie toggery.

In the morning light, the banality of the fashions hit Ed like a Pet Rock. 'Will the cast of *Hair* please come and pick up their wardrobe?' He turned to Pete. 'Okay, Fearless Leader, you first.'

---

[14] She habitually stole from the 'Take A Penny' dish, for example. This may seem out-of-character, but it wasn't. Sue Perversie walked around convinced that the worst fates she could imagine were just about to unfold, that meteors were inevitably aimed at her and it was only a matter of time before one got lucky. This, Sue felt, was just the way of the world. The best she could do in the face of it was occasionally goose her anxiety into a sort of fatalistic, still rather bleak, cheerfulness. With an outlook like that, one can see the appeal of the criminal life; she was simply too timid to get ambitious about it.

Pete balked; he had a secret fear of buttons. 'I'm still not sure I believe all this,' Pete said, swishing his cricket bat back and forth. 'Professor Berke says it's just hallucinations. No point in cramming in if it's just hallucinations.'

As voices echoed in the hallway outside, Ed gave Pete a hard push. 'Only one way to find out!' They all piled in before Pete could protest, and Ed pulled the door shut.

The four of them dropped to the ground, and began to crawl. It was easier to crawl under the clothes than to push through them, and one didn't run the risk of poking an eye out on a stick of incense protruding from a pocket.

'Ahh!' Pete yelled suddenly.

'What?' Sue asked.

'N-nothing,' Pete said. 'I thought I put my hand on a— eww, what is this puddle?'

'That's the drug-stuff,' Ed said.

'Whoops,' Pete said. 'I just crawled through it.'

Within moments, everybody's mind was freshly blown. It was bad enough to be cooped up with your older sister's bottom hovering there at close range, Ed thought, but when she turned into a water buffalo . . . The clothes brushing against their backs suddenly felt like the fringed rollers of a car wash, then the tentacles of a sea anemone. When they became fir trees, Loo announced from the back, 'Time to stand up.'

For the first time in Pete's life, sports didn't seem that important. 'I think I'm going to found an underground newspaper,' he said. His siblings were too deeply into their own trips to notice.

'Brr,' Sue said, shivering. 'How come you didn't tell us it was going to be bloody freezing?'

'Blame the author. I've found you really can't trust him at all, even on the most basic stuff,' Ed said. 'Two chapters ago, I was out here *forever* and he didn't even . . .' From the moment the words left Ed's mouth, he wanted to take them back. Now the others would know beyond any doubt that he, too, had been to Blarnia.

Luckily, the author was as inattentive as ever – the other children didn't even notice. 'I don't care how ridiculous I look,' Sue said. 'I'm putting on some of these clothes.' She put on a peasant blouse, then a tangerine velvet cape over that.

Ed pointed and laughed – then felt a chill breeze up his shorts. As flakes of snow danced in the air, he and the others swallowed their sartorial pride and picked some clothing off the rack. Pete wore a Nehru jacket in Day-Glo yellow. Not to be outdone, Ed slipped on a satin Sergeant Pepper-style suit in peacock blue. But Loo topped them all, snagging a fringed buckskin jacket with 'Capricorn' in beadwork on the back.

'*I'm* a Capricorn. It's like I was fated to wear this,' Loo said spacily.

'Unquestionably,' Ed said ironically. He noted that Loo was even more annoying under the influence of controlled substances; he didn't mind them all trying to expand their minds, it was just that Pete, Sue and Loo had so far to go. 'What other explanation could there *possibly* be for it?'

'I know, it's totally far out!' Sarcasm was the first thing that died during mind-expansion. 'Let's pretend we're hippies.'

'Pretending and having a mass hallucination?' Sue said. 'Whoa— meta.'

'Well, we have to pick something to do,' Ed said. 'Time passes slower back in the other place. We have to spend hours and hours here just to avoid the inspectors.' Ed knew what he wanted to do, go to the Wide Witch's house as fast as his mostly hairless legs could carry him, but he didn't know how to convince the others. 'Anybody have any ideas?'

'I dunno,' Pete said. 'Something mellow.'

Sue and Ed turned in amazement. 'Pete' and 'mellow' didn't inhabit the same Universe. But then again, who would've thought that their little straight-arrow sister Loo would get into astrology?

'Let's go to Mr Dumbness' pad,' Loo said. 'He's cool.'

They all followed Loo. It wasn't far, but it took them forever; suddenly the whole idea of walking in straight lines seemed 'totally Fascist.'

Pete stopped. 'Is that a squirrel wearing a bird costume?' he asked.

'Shut up!' the squirrel hissed. 'You'll blow my cover.'

'Oh,' Pete said, slapping the squirrel five. 'Sorry, lil' dude.'

The chill and the walk began to lessen the drug's effect; the hormones, too, seemed to be receding. It was a lucky thing, too – Pete's shirt had been chafing his nipples like the dickens.

The children got to a little hollow in the woods. Loo suddenly stopped. 'Here it is,' she said.

'Here what is?' Sue asked. 'I mean, there is no 'here' and 'there,' the whole duality trip is an illusion, I concede that. But what are we supposed to be looking at?'

'Mr Dumbness' cave,' Loo said. 'It's well-hidden.'

'I'll say,' Ed carped. 'How the heck do we get in it?'

'Everybody has to bang their heads on that rock,' Loo said. 'That's the only way Mr Dumbness ever finds it – he says you have to be a little woozy. Pete, you probably don't have to.'

'That's okay,' Pete said, slamming his noggin into the rock. 'I . . . like it . . .'

'I don't have to, either,' Loo said. 'Mr Dumbness says I'm a natural.'

One minute and several newly-bruised brains later, the Perversie children stood at the door to Mr Dumbness' cave. Only there was no door, not any more. Mr Dumbness' cave had been trashed; all the bookcases had been pulled down, all the crockery smashed, even the steam-powered DVD had been taken to pieces and scattered around the room.

'Tsk-tsk,' Sue clucked. Tidiness really *meant* something to her.[15]

'Wow,' Ed said. 'You never said Mr Dumbness was a college student.'

'It wasn't like this before,' Loo said. 'He's very tidy. He got very cross when I threw up on his rug.'

Sue gave a small, strangled cry.

'I can't imagine why,' Pete said.

'Oh well,' Ed said. 'No sense crying over a spilt life.' He began sifting through the mess, looking for something valuable to loot. 'Ooh, look!' Pete picked up the

---

[15] She even combed her spaghetti before eating it.

The Chronicles of Blarnia

painting of Fauns playing poker. 'Think I can get anything for this on eBuy?'

'Ed!' Loo cried. 'You can't just steal Mr Dumbness' belongings.'

'Well, whose belongings do you want me to steal, then?'

'But he's my friend,' Loo pleaded.

'Ed . . .' Sue said, a bit scoldingly.

'Look, Loo, there are some things more important in life than friends. Money, for example. With money, you can buy all the friends you want.'

'Don't get upset,' Pete said, putting his arm around his little sister. 'Swiping stuff is simply part of establishing a new colony, Loo. It's a tradition – the natives expect it. In fact, they get pretty cheesed-off when you *don't* do it.'

Loo shook off her brother's encircling arm and stomped away.

Ed got a brainwave. 'I have an idea,' he said, trying to betray no special interest. 'We could go and see the Wide Witch. She's not a friend of Loo's, so I could steal from her – we all could. And she's a Queen, so I bet she has lots of nice stuff.'

'A Queen, eh? Maybe she'll make me a knight!' Toadying always seemed to give Pete's face an almost holy illumination. Pete stood for a second, finger on lips; he felt a tickle of thought somewhere in his oft-fractured skull. Finally, it fell out of his mouth. 'Right – I know what we'll do.' He dropped to the floor, and pulled up a corner of Mr Dumbness's carpet. Scurrying underneath, he flipped the carpet over himself. 'Now somebody put debris on me!' came a muffled voice.

'Pete, what on earth are you doing?' Ed said with exasperation.

'I'm going to hide here – lying in wait!' the Pete-lump said, then sneezed. 'Excuse me. Dusty.'

Sue sighed. 'You can tell a lot about someone from how clean it is under their carpets.'

The Pete-lump continued. 'Then, when this Dumbness chap returns, we'll spring. Once he's enslaved, we can get him to help cart all the stuff away from this Queen's place.'

'I don't know, Pete,' Sue said. 'It seems so . . . rude, especially since she's royalty and everything.'

'Why?' Ed said, incensed. He was already hunting for the heaviest thing he could find to put on top of Pete. 'It's a perfectly good plan. You're such a goody-goody.'

'I am not, and besides' – Sue held up a piece of paper – 'I don't think Mr Dumbness is coming back.'

'Oh no!' Loo said, rushing over and snatching the paper away from her sister.

What did the paper say? Everyone, including the lump, looked at her expectantly. Loo, never a steady reader, made something up. 'Dear Loo,' she intoned. 'How are you? I am fine. If anyone tries to steal my stuff, you can kick them.' She ran over and kicked the lump.

'Ow! Why didn't you kick Ed?'

'Because Ed can run and you can't,' Loo said, kicking again as her eldest brother squirmed frantically.

'Let me have that,' Sue said, taking the piece of paper.

Pete threw the carpet back and hauled himself to his feet. He glared at Loo. 'You're gonna get it!' As Pete chased Loo around the cave waving his cricket bat, Sue read aloud:

'Woof woof woof Mr Dumbness woof woof treason woof woof woof Her Hugeness the Queen woof woof woof woof. Woof, woof woof woof come and get him, if you're not chicken.
    Signed,
    Furious Arf
    Captain of the Secret (woof) Police.
    WOOF WOOF WOOF QUEEN!'

'Boy, is *that* lame,' Ed said. 'Why would anybody

leave a document just lying around? There has to be a more clever way to move the story along.'

'Now, don't make fun of the plotting,' Sue said. 'I'm sure the author is doing the best he can.'[16]

Once they got back outside (Ed couldn't stop himself from pocketing a few items on the way out), the children suddenly realized that wanting to find Mr Dumbness and actually doing it were two different things entirely. Luckily for this poorly constructed story, there was a plot device sitting on a snowy branch nearby.

'Look!' Loo said. 'It's a robin!'

'Wearing a hat!' Pete said.

'That's flashing a message!' Ed said.

Sue chimed in. 'Which reads "Plot Device . . . Follow Me"!'

There was a pause. 'So what do we do now?' Loo asked.

Ed refused to answer the question – how else would the rest of them learn? The robin swooped closer and closer, trying to catch their attention. Pete tried to hit it with his bat, but the bird deftly avoided his swipes. It stuck its tongue out at the grumbling meathead.

'Since when do robins have tongues?' Loo asked.

[16] Yeah, right.

'I'm not going to tell you again about the author,' Sue scolded.

Ed took charge. 'Pete, stop bothering that bird and come back over here. We need to *think*.' As the Perversie children huddled, trying to figure out how to find out where Mr Dumbness had been taken, they did not notice the robin's feverish attempts to attract their attention.

Playing dumb, Ed had extracted one of Mr Dumbness' cloven running shoes, and was forcing Loo to sniff it. 'Think like a bloodhound,' he said in an encouraging voice.

Finally someone noticed the incredible commotion being kicked up by the robin. It had been squawking, buzzing their heads, and had even lit a small fire.

'Thank you, Mr Robin!' Ed said, thoroughly enjoying the bird's frustration. 'I had no idea robins could flap that fast.'

'Yes, thank you. We'll be ever so much more comfortable now,' Sue said, turning back to discussing Pete's suggestion, which rather predictably involved high explosives. 'But where shall we get the C-four, Pete?'

Pete shrugged. 'I'm an ideas man,' he said, scratching his head with his bat.

The robin cleared its throat, and tapped Sue's foot with its beak.

Michael Gerber

'I think he wants a tip,' Ed said, pointing. 'For the fire, perhaps.'

'Sorry little fellow,' Sue said kindly. 'I'm tapped out.'

The robin gave a small scream of frustration. Whatever they were paying him, it wasn't enough. He ran up to Ed's leg and kicked it.

The robin began hopping in the snow, as if it were having some sort of grand mal-category mental event. Ed looked down. 'The animals here are dreadfully high-strung,' he said.

'You guys, you guys,' Loo said, 'I think it's trying to tell us something. Look! It's writing in the snow!'

The robin was indeed making words out of its skinny footprints. 'FOLLOW ME, YOU ANORAKS,' it wrote.

'I am not!' Loo said, extra-mad because it hit home. The bird refused to engage in debate.

'Birds!' Pete said wearily. 'It's always *Twenty Questions* with them. Never just come out with what they mean.'

'You can say that again,' Ed agreed with a sigh.

'That's not fair,' Sue said. As the Perversies splintered into a loud, fractious discussion of sex roles, specifically to what degree male and female behaviour was innate and what was learned from society, the robin saw his brief window of communication closing once again. Desperate, he flew to a branch high above Ed's head, aimed, and _____.

Ed felt the outrage hit squarely, and slip down the back of his head. As boys his age are wont to do in such situations, he gathered a snowball, hiding a sizeable rock in the middle. Ed threw it as hard as he could, but missed.

The robin flew off. Ed took off after him, pausing to gather and hurl inaccurate snowballs. 'I knew (unh!) – what you wanted – all the (unh!) time!'

The others followed, laughing their heads off.

CHAPTER 7

 The children followed the robin deeper and deeper into the snowy forest. Everyone was getting quite hungry, and so began looking at the robin not simply as a way to find Mr Dumbness, but as a refreshing repast – if they could only catch him. After Pete tried to grab him, the robin made a rude gesture and flew off.

'Great,' Loo said, untying her bib. 'Now what are we to do?'

The children sat on a log, depressed and unsure of their next move. As their bottoms chilled, they turned on each other almost immediately.

Naturally, Ed's thoughts turned to cannibalism, and he began to decide which of his siblings would be the most delectable. Pete was surely too tough. Sue was too old, and even though her beard was almost gone, all that extra testosterone probably made her stringy – good for stew, perhaps, but not al fresco. That left Loo, who sat on the log's end picking her nose, blissfully unaware. So young, so delicious, Ed thought . . . She'll probably thank me for it, too . . . Suddenly, the drooling boy saw something out of the corner of his eye – and it looked edible! 'Hey, nice beaver!' Ed said.

Sue clouted him. 'Language!'

'No, really!' Ed said, pointing.

Sue didn't see, but Loo did. 'It looks so furry and warm!'

'LOO!' Sue said, genuinely shocked.

'What?' Loo ducked, Sue swung and missed.

Pete saw it and joined in. 'I have to say that's the nicest beaver I've ever seen . . .'

'The only one you've ever seen,' Ed quipped.

'You are all filthy beasts!' Sue said. 'Just because Mum and Dad aren't here – I'd like to see how *you'd* like to be related to you! You're doing this just to torment – oh.' She finally saw it. '*That* beaver. I thought you were talking about . . . forget it.'

The plump, brown creature looked around as if to make sure nobody was watching, then motioned for the children to approach. When the children made no movement , the irritated beaver stood up on its hind legs, and threw its paws up in the air in a gesture of 'what the hell are you waiting for?'

'Oh my God!' Sue said. 'That's not a normal beaver! It must be some sort of mutant-zombie-devil!' Sue got terrified when things didn't act as they should.

The beaver shook its head in frustration, then began walking towards them. Sue freaked out.

'It's coming towards us – Pete, do something! Kill it! KILL IT!'

'All right,' Pete said, smacking his cricket bat into his palm and striding forward. He didn't think that violence could solve every problem, but it was always fun giving it a shot.

'Don't smush it so badly we can't eat it,' Ed called after his brother.

Pete gave a nod and a grunt. 'C'mere, Mr Beaver . . .'

The beaver saw Pete's intentions and scurried under a large evergreen. Pete swore and gave chase. The rest of the children followed.

'So now we're following a beaver?' Ed said. 'I didn't come here to trail after a whole menagerie!'

'So stay here,' Loo said. She was frankly pretty sick of Ed's attitude. He didn't appreciate Blarnia.

When the children trooped under the skirt of the tree, they saw the beaver standing over by the trunk. Pete took a swing. Quick as a flash, the beaver grabbed the wooden bat between its long yellow incisors and held on. Dropping to all fours for better purchase, the beaver levered Pete into the air. Pete screamed with a voice still high like a girl's, as the beaver slung him this way and that. As Pete's siblings laughed unhelpfully, the beaver slammed the boy into the branches and ground until it was clear he knew who was boss. The beaver spat out the bat and Pete fell to the forest floor.

'Wasn't really trying,' Pete sniffed.

'You've got pine needles sticking in your bottom,' Loo said.

'Hello,' the beaver whispered. 'It's safe to talk here – this tree has been swept for listening devices. But they could be using parabolic mikes from remote locations, so please keep your voices—'

'IT TALKS!' Sue screamed. 'THE _____ BEAVER TALKS! PETE, YOU GOTTA—' Sue passed out from fear.

'Not good following directions, is she?' the beaver said. 'Are you the Sons and Daughters of Atom and Steve?'

While still conscious, the two boys were having a little trouble with the idea of polite conversation with a quadruped. Loo, who was used to living in a world of her own idiocy, took it in stride.

'That's us!' she said brightly. 'We're looking for my friend Mr Dumbness. He's making me a mix tape.'

The beaver chuckled. 'Same old Dumbness. He's made one for every female in Blarnia. Doesn't matter what species, old or young, whether they're straight or not . . .'

Pete's protectiveness kicked in. 'If that goat even laid a hand on my sister . . .'

'I'm sure nothing happened,' the beaver said. 'He's socially quite awkward. It's sad, really – Dumbness is the only satyr I know who's still a virgin. There's talk of revoking his licence.'

'This is bullcrap,' Ed said. 'I'm walking back.'

'No!' Loo said. 'I want my mix tape!' She turned to the beaver. 'My brother doesn't mean to be rude, Mr Beaver—'

'*Ms* Beaver.'

'Sorry – Ms Beaver. It's just that we're hungry.'

'Then follow me to my home. We'll have a fine dinner, and I'll give you the tape he gave me. I never listen to it.'

Sue was stirring. After she had been talked down from her pure, unreasoning terror, Ms Beaver gathered them all close, so close that one of her whiskers went up Ed's nostril. 'Sorry.' Placing a paw on her belly and making a face, she whispered, 'They say Asthma is on the move – or maybe I ate some green wood.'

At the mention of Asthma's name, each of the children felt a very special feeling. It was like – it's hard to explain, but once you've felt this feeling, you'll never,

ever forget it. It felt sort of like being tricked, only nicer, and sort of like being talked down to, only more serious. It was the feeling of someone trying to convince you to believe in a certain religion, but thinking that you couldn't possibly understand unless they told you a long, only marginally interesting story that constantly compared Jesus to idiotic things like delicious cake, or summer holidays. They agreed with Ms Beaver – it was all a little sick-making.

After his stomach returned to normal, Ed got an idea. Sticking his fingers in his ears, he shouted, 'Asthma!' Everyone turned a little green. 'Asthma! Asthma Asthma Asthma!'

'Quit!' Loo said, hitting him. Ed shrugged it off and kept chanting.

'Really, stop.' Sue said. 'I'm going to hurl.'

'Okay, okay. I'll stop,' Ed said, pleased as punch.

Pete glowered at him. 'You'd better.'

Well, as anybody who's ever had a sibling knows, Ed couldn't let that pass. Taking a deep breath, he said, 'As—'

Pete grabbed Ed's collar and drew him close, the better to punch him.

'—mara.'

'Oh.' Pete let him down.

'I was about to say "Asmara's warmer than this." It's

the capital of Eritrea, in Northern Ethiopia, population a hundred and twenty thousand,' Ed said, feigning ignorance. 'What did you think I was going to say? As—'

Pete grabbed him again.

'—thenosphere? It's just a zone within the earth some distance below the surface, which consists of material subject to plastic deformation, underlying the stronger librosphere.'

Pete let him go again.

'I have no idea why hearing about that would bother you,' Ed said, sauntering away. 'Were you afraid I would say . . . *Asthma*?'

Pete chased the cackling Ed all around the tree.

'Quiet! Quiet!' Ms Beaver said, tugging the hot pink forelock she always had the hairdresser put in. Ms Beaver had a right to be nervous; with every imprecation from Pete or laugh from Ed, escape got that much more difficult; the Wide Witch's minions were evil, but they weren't deaf.

'If you don't shut up,' Ms Beaver hissed, 'we'll be caught for sure!' Ed trotted by, giggling, and she grabbed him. 'Young man, do you want molten lead put up your bum?'

'Let me think.' Ed gathered himself, and thought for a second; so many questions were trick ones. 'Erm . . . no,' he said.

Ms Beaver walked out of the skirt of the tree. 'Then follow me,' she said. 'And be *quiet*!'

The children shambled after. Loo was sharpening a pine cone, but couldn't get it sharp enough to puncture skin.

'Asthma,' Ed whispered to Pete, then scampered away. Pete quietly body-slammed him into a snowdrift.

They followed the beaver through the forest for a long time. After about an hour, Sue dropped back to talk to the boys. 'Does anyone else find it odd that this animal talks?' she asked.

'Does anybody else feel like hurling every time they hear the A-word?' Ed asked. ('Arse?' Loo offered, but nobody paid attention.) 'Actually,' Ed continued, 'that seems to be wearing off a bit.'

Ed, ever the rationalist, guessed that it was the drugs. 'Between living in the Professor's house and crawling through that banana peel stuff, who knows what's happening to our brains?' He imagined his own, huddled up against the back of his skull, quivering and whimpering.

Loo overheard them. 'Since my brain is already ruined, can I have cider now?' she asked Sue.

'I suppose,' Sue said. 'Seems rather pointless to say no.'

'Goody!' Next stop, alcohol poisoning.

Ms Beaver turned and told the girls to be quiet. Their tongues had just reentered their mouths when Ms Beaver stopped suddenly; she seemed to be pondering something.

'I'm not banging my head against another rock,' Ed whispered to Pete defiantly.

'Wuss,' Pete whispered back.

Ms Beaver tapped her long incisors with a paw-nail. 'How hungry is everybody?'

'Very!' all the children said, except for Ed, who boomed, 'Ravenous!' Ed felt that the occasional big word signalled him as a breed apart. Pete had his sports and made-up boarding school, Sue her knitting and work with the League of Boring Voters, and Loo – well, it was obvious Loo was unique.

'Shh! For Asthma's sake, do you want the Wide Witch to catch us?'

'Nooo-oo,' the children said, except for Ed, who said, 'Yes!' They all looked at him. 'Joking, joking, I was just joking!'

Ms Beaver didn't think she liked Ed. In fact, she didn't like any of them. Ah well, she said to herself, one can't choose one's fellow characters. She pointed to a large log. 'I think that'll do nicely. Ed, would you carry it for us?'

'Oh, no way,' Ed said, chuckling. He regarded all physical labor with a deep suspicion – it wasn't that he wouldn't do it ever, but hard experience had taught him that it usually wasn't worth it. 'I mean, I can't – I've got this trick . . . knuckle . . . But I'm sure Pete would be delighted to.'

'I'll do it!' Loo said. She ran over to the log, grabbed a couple of stubby branches that protruded from it, and heaved. It wouldn't budge, so Pete ambled over. Perhaps it was the angle, or a trick of the light, but Ms Beaver suddenly noticed that Pete's neck was much wider than his head.

'Stand aside,' he said. Pete handed his bat over to Sue, and began to drag the log. If anyone was following them, they now had a nice, straight line to guide them.

Seeing that Pete's hands were full – and he no longer held the bat – Ed got an idea. He waited until everyone relaxed, then sprang over and began forcing snow down the back of Pete's jacket. This was the signal for a general melee, where every old resentment could be expressed with ice and snow and partially frozen mud.

Ms Beaver lost it. '*Sons of Atom! Daughters of Steve!*' she said. 'The spies! The listening devices! The security cameras!'

'No security cameras here,' a badger said, its shutter clicking.

Ms Beaver grabbed at it, and missed. 'Ooh! That's it!' she yelled, then plopped down on the ground with an angry bottom. 'I refuse to be responsible for the rest of this chapter!' As the siblings beat on each other, Ms Beaver began writing her defence. Maybe she wouldn't need it, but she sure as heck wasn't going to be responsible if they all ended up as lawn ornaments.

Twenty minutes later, with sodden clothes in addition to scrapes and bruises, the Perversie children followed Ms Beaver to a frozen river.

'Careful, now,' Ms Beaver cautioned the bedraggled children. 'Go where I go, and slowly. It would be a shame if any of you fell in,' Ms Beaver said, not meaning it. If it was possible to actually *break* a river, these dreadful moppets could. Then they rounded a bend, and everyone saw an amazing sight.

Sue gasped. 'What is it?'

'It's a dam,' Pete said, in a know-it-allish tone. He'd have had a much better vocabulary if all words sounded like swears.

'Actually, we prefer the term "dyke,"' Ms Beaver said.

The structure was immense, a wedge of finely worked wood that stretched at least ten storeys into the sky. At the bottom, there were ports for water to rush out, but only a trickle could be seen.

'There's a lake behind there,' Ms Beaver said. 'Sixteen-hundred acres. Normally, it could generate ten million kilowatts of electricity a year. If everything wasn't frozen solid, that is. And all the machinery is made of wood, that's also a problem. But I'm working on it – Blarnia can't grow if it doesn't have electricity.'

'I think it's wonderful,' Loo said, utterly charmed. She'd seen a show on electric chairs once.

'Be sure to tell my' – she looked at Peter; guys like him worried her – 'my roommate,' Ms Beaver said. 'She thinks I'm crazy. She'll be singing a different tune when I give her the microwave oven I'm working on. I just have to learn how to whittle the wiring thin enough.'

As the group walked up the side of the structure to Ms Beaver's cosy house perched atop it, Ed asked, 'How d'you do it? I mean, without thumbs, and everything?'

Ms Beaver lifted something from around her neck, and placed it on one of her paws. They had all assumed it was merely a very ugly sort of necklace, but it turned out to be a cunning arrangement of cords which held in place a stubby prosthetic thumb.

'Amazing,' Ed said.

'Thank you,' Ms Beaver said. 'I made it myself.'

Pete was whacking the side of the dam as he walked. 'Stop it!' Ms Beaver said. 'Give me that!' She wrestled the bat from him and threw it down to the river below.

Sue, Ed, and Loo tensed with excitement, ready for the showdown. Instead, Pete burst into tears.

'There, there,' Ms Beaver said, hugging him. 'It's all right. I'll carve you something better.'

'Something . . . pointy?' Pete said through his tears.

'If you like,' Ms Beaver said. 'Now pull yourself together and stop getting snot on my fur.' The group began walking again, and soon they were at the top. Using her fake thumb, Ms Beaver pointed to a tidy little mound perched atop the structure. 'Be it ever so humble, that's home.' She seemed to be waiting for someone to say something flattering.

'It looks small,' Ed said. 'Are you poor?'

Ms Beaver just turned and walked towards the house, muttering. She was seriously considering switching sides. The Wide Witch might be grabby and smell of fried food, but this lot was intolerable. Asthma offered good health insurance, but there were *limits*.

Waiting for Ms Beaver to get out of earshot, Sue hissed, '*Ed*! I can't believe you! That was incredibly rude!'

Ed wasn't listening – he was imagining that fine future day when he would swindle his siblings out of their inheritances. It wouldn't be much – but it was the thought that counted. Lost in this pleasant dream, Ed looked down the river. He saw a little valley between two great milky mounds, then between that lower down, another mound, wild and overgrown with foliage. That must be where the Wide Witch lived, he thought. He'd get them down there somehow. But how?

'Hey, does anybody want to go down that way with me?' Ed said. 'I think I see a McDonald's.'

'Get stuffed,' Pete mumbled, dragging the log past him towards the hut. After the 'Asthma' attack and the snow fight, Ed had used up his siblings' trust. He would have to use subterfuge.

At the door of the little hut, Ms Beaver turned to the children and said, 'I just want to let you know that Ruth's . . . different.' Sue gasped, and Ms Beaver hastened to explain. 'Not dangerous – just . . . different. You'll know it when you see it.' She unlocked the door, and opened it. 'Honey, we're here,' Ms Beaver called. 'Ruth, I brought the humans . . .'

Ruth the Beaver was a bit smaller and thinner than her mate, but what the Perversie children noticed was her hair, which had been formed into a massive constellation of dreadlocks.

'Oh God, Naomi,' Ruth said, in a husky smoker's voice. 'The house is a mess, there's nothing to eat and I just got the boys to sleep . . .'

'We think your house looks lovely,' Sue said.

'This dump?' Ruth rasped. 'You *must* be joking. Since you're here, sit down.'

Each of the children found a three-legged stool. As soon as they sat down, they found that each one was decidedly rickety. Loo fell off hers – one of the legs was so short that absolutely no weight could be put on it without the sitter being dumped on to the floor.

Ruth saw this; she was used to it. Without comment, she turned to Naomi. 'What am I supposed to feed these little weasels?'

'Humans, dear. Sons of Atom and Daughters of Steve.' Naomi pointed at each gender in turn. 'Don't worry, we got a take-away on the way home,' Naomi said, with a sort of desperate cheerfulness. She nudged Pete.

'Here,' Pete said, dragging the log over to Ruth, who regarded him (and it) coolly. Halfway there, Pete decided to drop it on Ed's foot, accidentally on-purpose. Ed howled.

'Now you've done it,' Ruth said. 'The boys are awake!' She rushed into the next room.

'I don't hear anything,' Loo whispered to Naomi.

'Don't just stand there,' Ruth called to her mate. 'Help me!'

Naomi, thoroughly henpecked, scampered into the

other room. Moments later, she and Ruth emerged, each holding a small log in their arms.

For once, even Ed was speechless.

'This is our son Woody,' Ruth said, tipping the log like a newborn, so that the children could see the crude face drawn on it. 'And that little shaver is Chip. Can you wave, Chip? Can you?'

Halfheartedly, Naomi shook the small sprig protruding from Chip's flank.

'What, are you joking?' Ed said gruffly. 'They're just—' Sue stamped on Ed's foot, the same one so recently under a log.

'I hope that leaves a mark!' Sue whispered to her brother. He was just so rude.

Pete laughed, so Ed stamped on his foot.

Desperate to prevent another all-out war, Naomi thought quickly. She pointed at the log in Ruth's arms and said, 'I think somebody's got a poopy nappy!'

Ruth raised Woody up in her arms, and rubbed her nose against the log. 'Who's got a poopy nappy? Poopy-doopy-doo!'

Ed, allergic to baby talk, felt his stomach heave. Sue, on the other hand, immediately bonded with Ruth. 'How sweet,' she murmured, and walked over to the beaver. 'I'm Sue. What a lovely little baby you have . . .'

'Thank you,' Ruth said. 'I think he looks like Naomi.'

'I don't know,' Sue said. 'I think there's a lot of you in there, too . . . Anyway, that's my sister Loo – Loo, stop trying to swallow that stool!'

'I wasn't,' Loo said, taking the leg out of her mouth.

'Forgive her, she's a little D-E-V-E-L-O-P-M-E-N-T-A-L-L-Y- . . .'

'I am not!' Loo said brattily.

'Not what?' Sue asked.

'Whatever you were spelling!'

Sue sighed, but refused to take the bait. Sometimes it was physically hard to be so mature. 'And the two blokes holding their feet are my brothers, Pete and Ed.'

'Hi,' Ed said.

'Hi,' Pete said. He spotted a twig on the floor. Wanting to be nice, he picked it up and said, 'Is this your dog, then? What breed is it?'

Ruth smiled weakly, then shot a glance at Naomi as if to say, 'That boy is crazy.'

CHAPTER 8

 Dinner was, quite predictably, a terribly painful experience for the Perversie children. The humans spent the better part of an hour gingerly mouthing the slabs of wood that had been cut into 'steaks' and placed in front of them.

'I gah anotha spl'n'er,' Loo said.

'I told you, chew slowly,' Sue said. Pete had the whole thing in his mouth and was trying unsuccessfully to tear out a chunk with his teeth. Ed had torn off a small scrap from the edge and was glumly trying to suck it for nourishment. Sue had pried off a bit of lichen from her section; Ed nearly leapt across the table to grab it from her, but found that he was too weak to do anything but swear softly under his breath.

As hungry as the Perversie children were, they had no right to expect that a pair of beavers would eat like humans, with meat and potatoes and tea and dairy products. How on earth would beavers get things like that? Do you think beavers run slaughterhouses? No self-respecting pig would put up with that for a second. And what do you think a cow would do if a beaver tried to milk it? That's right – the same thing *you'd* do if a beaver tried to milk *you*! You'd call a policeman, and no one would fault you for doing so. Ruth and Naomi were (like all of their species) strict vegetarians, and their propensity for serving guests cellulose *al dente* was infamous throughout Blarnia.

'We never entertain,' Ruth said, and now the children knew why.

'As soon as you're finished,' Naomi said, 'I'll tell you what happened to Mr Dumbness.'

'We're finished now!' the children chorused.

'I thought you were hungry,' Ruth said. 'You've hardly touched your food.'

'We're much too excited to hear what happened to . . . whatever his name was,' Ed said.

'Yeah,' Pete said, yawning.

'Somebody should tell her,' Naomi said, jabbing her fake thumb in the direction of Loo, who was racing around the table playing 'Duck, Duck, Goose.'

Sue leaned over. 'She doesn't know this, but she's only our H-A-L-F-S-I-S-T-'

Loo abruptly stopped running. 'I am not! Whatever you were spelling!'

The beavers once again felt like they were in the middle of an uncomfortable family affair. Naomi cleared her throat and said, 'Now, as to Mr Dumbness.'

'Yes?' Loo said expectantly.

'He's probably . . . erm . . . I mean, the most likely explanation is – of course we can't know for sure . . .' Loo was looking at her with big, hopeful eyes. The beaver couldn't dash the poor waif's dreams, not yet. 'He's probably living with a family out in the country. On a farm. With lots of other little Fauns to play with.'

'That's surprising,' Ed said. 'I'd figured he was dead.'

'Ed!' Sue scolded.

'My friend is not dead!' Loo said, offended.

'Wanna bet?' Ed said. 'Twenty quid that Mr What's-his-face has already been planted. Pete, mark it down.'

'All right,' Pete said. As the oldest, and the one big enough to make everybody pay up, Pete was the official bookie of the Perversie children. 'Let's go and find him and see.'

'Oh, no, you couldn't do that,' Naomi said. 'He's at the castle of the Wide Witch, and no one's allowed in there.'

'We could sneak in,' Pete said. 'I say we dig a tunnel . . .'

'I wouldn't,' Ruth said. 'The Wide Witch is the nastiest person around.'

'Come now,' Ed said, 'surely that's a little unfair? What could she possibly do to us? I mean, we're tourists.'[17]

---

[17] Actually, they had student visas.

'She could eat you, for starters. Or sit on you, if her jaws were tired,' Ruth said.

'God knows they should be,' Naomi said.

Ruth nodded. 'She could even turn you into butter and spread you on toast.'

'No, children. Best to let Asthma handle it. If Mr Dumbness can be saved, Asthma'll do it.' Naomi paused for dramatic effect. 'They say he's on the move.'

'On the move?' Ruth said. 'I bloody well hope he's on the move – right to here, so he can fix this chair he made for us!' She plopped into her rocking chair, one side of which was fully six inches shorter than the other.

'I told you,' Naomi said in a tired voice, 'he doesn't do carpentry any more.'

'He'll effing well do some when I see him!' Ruth said. 'I mean, look!' She started rocking, and began doing circles around the room. 'It's ridiculous! We paid him good money!'

'We'll talk about this later,' Naomi said.

'And the bookcase in the hall!' Ruth said. 'It's a menace. I don't know why he didn't use nails, like a proper carpenter.'

'I *told* you why,' Naomi said. 'He has bad memories.'

'I'll give you a bad memory: me falling out of a rocking chair and being killed by an avalanche of books!'

'Have you finished? Have you finished bickering in front of our guests?'

'. . . Some people think just because they're the Messiah . . .' Ruth mumbled, as she cleared the table.

'Thank you.' Naomi launched back into the previous conversation. 'As I was saying, you let Asthma take care of Mr Dumbness.'

The Perversie children shrugged as one.

'I got my tape,' Loo said, satisfied.

Naomi seemed confused. 'Aren't you going to ask me about Asthma? What he's like? Turn-ons are: sunsets and world peace; turn-offs are haircuts and mean people.'

Ruth sneered. 'Naomi has a crush on Asthma.'

'Please stop,' Pete said. 'Every time you say his name, I throw up a little in my mouth.'

'Me, too,' Sue said. 'Ugh, sap.' She made a face. 'Acid reflux, the gift that keeps on giving.'

'Anyway, why should we care about . . . that person?' Loo asked. 'It's not like we need carpentry.'

'Because he's the hero of the book, that's why!' the beaver said with irritation.

'I thought *I* was the hero of the book,' Pete said.

'As if,' Ed said. 'You can't even *read*.'

'ENOUGH!' Naomi said. 'You children never let up.' She turned to her partner. 'See what I have to deal with?'

Ruth wasn't having it. 'I think this chair is giving me scoliosis,' she rasped.

Seeing that she was on her own, Naomi continued. 'Asthma' – Loo made a little gagging sound *sotto voce* – 'oh, come on, the name's not that bad. You'd better get used to it, because he's coming tomorrow.'

'Oh, what's the big deal?' Ruth said. 'He's just a house cat.'

Naomi's mouth fell open. 'I'm telling Asthma you said that!'

'So what? I don't care, he's your boyfriend, not mine.'

'He's not my—He'll wither you,' Naomi said. 'He did that once.'

'That's apocryphal,' Ruth sniffed.

'You better hope so,' Naomi said.

'I'm not scared. I doubt he's even coming.' Ruth lit up another cigarette. 'I think it's a metaphor.'

'Oh, you do, do you?' Ruth asked.

'Yeah,' the beaver said, brushing a stray dreadlock from her eyes. 'After somebody's been saying, "I'll be back any moment now," for two thousand years, I think it's pretty safe to assume that, yeah, they're speaking metaphorically.'

Naomi, nervously tugging her pink forelock again, turned to the children. 'Don't listen to her. We'll meet him tomorrow at the Stone Bathtub, and you can see for yourself whether Asthma is a metaphor or not. There's an old rhyme people say in these parts—' Naomi stopped and turned to her mate. 'I suppose it's too much to ask for you to beatbox?'

'Are you kidding?' Ruth said, rolling her eyes. 'This is how you ruined our last dinner party.'

Naomi made a face, then began to chant,

'You better watch out, you better not cry,
You better not pout, I'm telling you why,
Asthma—'

'*Cough—* copyright! copyright!— *cough*,' Ruth leapt in.

'This is all tremendously exciting,' Sue said, yawning broadly, 'but whatever has it to do with us?'

'Strangely enough, there's another old rhyme that deals with that very issue,' Naomi said. This time she sang a tune of her own invention.

'When four English children of appropriate classes,

(For Cair Amel only accommodates the finest of arses)

Park their fat bottoms on the throne

This limping dog of a book will be done.

Kings? Queens? One can't blame readers from becoming conceited

If you tell them stories full of such [expletive deleted]!'

At the mention of class, Sue naturally thought of her brother Ed. She looked around. 'Speaking of [expletive deleted], where's Ed?'

'Yeah,' Pete said. 'It's time for his thumping.' Pete had an internal body clock for such matters.

'You wouldn't think that an author would just let a character wander off like that,' Loo said. 'Seems like a cheap trick to move the plot along.'

'In this book,' Sue grumbled, 'nothing surprises me any more.'

'It was your rapping,' Ruth said. 'It drove him away.'

'It wasn't!' Naomi said, offended. 'As soon as I saw that kid, I thought, "He's been had by the Wide Witch."'

'Ahh, everything bad that happens, you blame it on the Wide Witch. "Oh, still Winter, must be the Witch," "Can't find any decent mud today, must be the Witch," "Eczema on my tail's back, must be the Witch", "Pizza's burned, must be —"'

'YOU HAVE PIZZA?' Pete exclaimed. 'We've been eating wood and you have pizza?'

'Gimme! Gimme! Gimme!' Loo said.

'It's wood, too,' Naomi said, and all the excitement left the room.

Her partner wouldn't let up. 'Stop blaming this —' she moved her paws to denote quote marks '—"Wide

Witch" for everything. Take some responsibility for your life!'

'So how do you explain why it's been winter for freakin' years?'

Ruth thought for a second. 'A slow moving high pressure front.'

'That's insane!' Naomi said, really losing her temper. The Perversies were really enjoying this – it was nice to be the audience for once, and not the spectacle. 'Look, I have my problems, but at least I don't traipse around pretending a couple of logs are my children!'

All the colour drained out of Ruth's face, no mean feat for a rodent covered with thick brown fur. 'I can't believe you said that,' she said quietly. 'Thank goodness Chip and Woody didn't hear you.'

'Ahh!' Naomi yelled. 'They're logs! Lumber! Wood! Like your head!'

'Oh, now you've done it,' Ruth said. 'You've woken them up! Don't listen to her, boys, she was just joking!' She rushed into the other room.

Naomi stormed over to the door. 'C'mon, you punks. First, we're heading to the backyard still, then we're going to meet Asthma.'

And that's exactly what they did.

CHAPTER 9

 I suppose you'll be wanting to know what happened to Ed. Well, if we must . . .

It was simple really: at a certain point, the boy's ravenous hunger affected his mind, so that whenever he looked over at one of the party chatting away listlessly in the beavers' snug-if-slightly-fetid home, all he saw was a giant cartoon turkey leg floating in midair. This was bad enough, but when the turkey legs all began dancing around his head, throwing gravy-drenched stuffing at each other whilst giggling like inebriated teenagers, Ed was faced with a difficult decision.

On the one hand, he could attack someone and eat them. This was certainly what he wanted to do, but it presented problems. It is a fact of life that once someone has seen you attack and eat another human being, they tend to trust you less. Oh, they may say that they don't see you in 'that way' any more, that they've totally forgotten the sight of you raving and slobbering, covered with grue, but prejudice is inevitable. Ed knew that if he gave in and ate someone now – even Loo! –

there was no chance of ever getting the rest of them to come and visit the Wide Witch.

Or Ed could flee to the Wide Witch himself.

The soundness of this scheme was obvious. Despite all the nasty things that people had been saying about the Wide Witch, she was the only person in this entire country (or alternate reality, or whatever it was – Ed didn't much care at the moment) one could be reasonably sure had something to eat. Everybody else in this bum-chilling stick-strewn heck-hole seemed to be talking animals, or even worse entirely mythological; and while Ed had once eaten a mouthful of straw for a bet, he had no desire to do it again. The Wide Witch seemed to like him – or something, girls could be so difficult to understand, especially when they weren't human and seemed kind of, erm, evil – but if it came to it, Ed felt sure he could exist for days just on the scraps that had fallen and been lost between her many flabby folds.

Ed considered inviting his siblings along, then decided against it. Yes, they might see the logic of his plan – but they were all so illogical in their ways, and would probably prevent him from going, just out of spite. Pete would sleep the entire night sitting on Ed's chest, he had done that before when Ed wanted to go and see a film Pete felt was too old for him. Anyway, Ed thought to himself, who wanted to share? The Queen is my special friend, Ed thought, and that was that.

Of course it's utterly absurd that Ed would've been able to sneak out of the Beavers' small house, even if there had been some curtains or a grandfather clock or a full-size reproduction of the Bayeux Tapestry or anything else to hide behind, which there wasn't. But for the sake of the story let's say he did it, all right?

As Naomi the beaver went into her rap, Ed quietly slipped out of the door and into the chilly night. As usual in this book, it was somehow cold enough to snow, but not cold enough to send Ed right back inside, cursing. Blarnia was truly a magical land, where characters could sometimes be forced to wear thick fur coats, and other times be able to walk around in street clothes for hours without complaint.

Unfortunately for Ed, this time it was tending towards cold. As he walked down the dam and then along the river, he cursed the hippies for not being more outdoorsy. His Sergeant Pepper jacket shone beautifully in the moonlight, but did a fairly lousy job of keeping him warm.

His breath whitening the air in front of him, Ed practised a few pick-up lines. 'Hi! I was just in the neighbourhood—' Was that good? No! She'd know he was lying. 'You know how you told me to come by and see you?' That wouldn't work either. She hadn't actually said that, and anyway, it would bring up the fact that he was coming alone, when she had specifically asked him to bring Idiots on Parade. He should just be honest. 'Do you want to . . . maybe . . . go out?' As Ed said this, his voice cracked a bit, causing a bubble of embarrassment and anxiety to form in his chest. Somewhere, off in the distance, an owl hooted. It sounded like laughter.[18]

'This is never going to work!' Ed said angrily. 'She's going to make fun of me!'

He looked back. The beavers' house was nowhere to be seen. And he was so hungry . . . Ed decided to press on. To cheer himself up, he started to think about the things he and 'Queenie' – that was the nickname he was going to give her – would do, once they were 'going out.' Actually all the people he knew that were 'going out' mostly still hung around with their regular friends, except for when whole groups of people went to films, or played video games at somebody's house after school. Pete talked about all the things that he and his girlfriend, Victoria Francoise, did when they met in the Chunnel (she was French), but Ed was beginning to

---

[18] And it was. That species of owl is known for its unkind sense of humour.

believe she didn't even exist, especially after he caught Pete giving himself a neck-hickey with the vacuum cleaner.

It was spooky out in the woods, and Ed had to keep a firm hold of his fear as he walked. The moonlight tended to throw grotesque shadows, fertile ground indeed for a boy of Ed's imagination. Every so often the boy thought he detected movement in the woods, which naturally led to the question: Did Blarnia have serial killers? If so, they were probably something incredibly fruity, like a hedgehog in a hockey mask. Quite unbidden, the image of Frog and Toad, working as a gay thrill-kill team, sprang into Ed's head. He shuddered, then tried to put it out of his mind by asking aloud, 'Do you think the Wide Witch has video games? She seems the sort of person who might.' His voice sounded so small and weak that hearing it aloud scared him even more.

By now there was as much snow inside Ed's shoes as there was feet. Hidden, half-buried roots, slippery, pointed sticks and every small jutting rock seemed to be conspiring together to trip him. He felt his thighs going numb, and suddenly his future came to him in a flash: he was going to die out here. Luckily, Ed had reserves that he was not aware of, most notably immense stores of resentment, which can in a pinch keep the body going for days. Ed began to really hate his siblings, especially Loo for discovering this crappy world in the first place, and Sue, for not letting them escape the Professor's house straight away, and finally Pete, simply because he was so bloody hearty and brutal all the time. He didn't want to die without ever having reached second base! *Was that fair?*

His head full of glum plans of how best to arrange his body to insult whoever found it, Ed turned a bend in the river . . . and there it was, the Wide Witch's home. It was, frankly, a little tacky. Oh, it was a castle, all right, and there was a certain plodding grandeur to that. But even in the dramatic moonlight, the total effect was that of a slightly down-at-the-heels medieval theme restaurant. The stone was a dull, uniform grey, and even in the gloom Ed could see that it was simply moulded concrete. Even the spires looked shop-bought. At least there were garden gnomes in the courtyard, Ed thought. Clichéd but fun.

As Ed approached the castle, trying to ignore the snow now inside his very socks, the boy saw that the figures in the courtyard weren't garden gnomes at all, but woodland creatures in various poses of defiance and flight. Ed laughed at the expressions on the faces of some of the statues – that Faun looked like it was soiling itself! Was that Loo's friend?

Ed examined it closer, trying to gather a few details in order to tease Loo more effectively. As he approached the statue of the Faun, Ed lost his balance on a slick patch. Quite instinctively, he reached for the statue's arm to keep from falling, and found that his fingers sunk right into it! It clearly wasn't stone. Ed brought his fingers to his nose, then to his mouth – it was butter-cream icing!

He set upon the statue like a wild animal, eating the now-mangled arm clean up to the shoulder. Stepping back, he gazed at the Faun. 'Looks ridiculous with just the one arm,' Ed said. 'I'll eat the other, just to even him out.'

The sweet, cloying icing soon made him both hyper and a little nauseous, so he moved to another statue, in hopes that it wasn't so rich. Ed had consumed a stoat, three voles and most of a fox when he heard a sound. It was a steady 'yip-yip-yip,' like an extremely annoying machine gun – and it seemed to be coming this way. Ed crouched behind a giraffe, eyes trained on the nearest corner of the castle. To his horror, he saw a huge shadow thrown against the snow – one of a hound it appeared, but a canine much bigger and fiercer than any hound Ed had encountered.

'Ahhhhh!' Yelling, the boy began to run around the palace, looking for a way in. The yipping did not cease, instead taking on a decidedly more frenzied quality once the chase was afoot. If only it had been a homicidal amphibian in a hockey mask, Ed thought bitterly. At least that would've been quieter.

Whether it was the lack of food, or simply the sedentary lifestyle of the overthoughtful child, Ed soon felt his wind giving out. Desperate, with burning lungs and a stitch in his side, he rounded the final corner of the castle. There – an open door! He skittered inside, hoping that the dog would not be smart enough to chase him.

There were more statues in here, also of buttercream. Hiding himself behind a sad-eyed rhino with a bite out of his backside, Ed peered at the open doorway. The yips grew closer, then closer still, until the fierce creature stood there, hackles up and menacing in the moonlight.

'What the _____?' Ed said, standing up. It was a toy Yorkshire terrier, no bigger than a large man's idea of a sandwich, and just as deadly. Ed moved forward intending to kick it, when the dog spoke in a piping voice.

'Who – yip! – are you? And why do you so – yip! – boldly gnaw on my – yap! – mistress' statues?' It was Furious Arf, the fearsome Captain of the Guard. Furious wasn't fearsome at all, but he was a big believer in positive thinking. Still, the toy Yorkshire terrier weighed less than a stapler, and couldn't shred a piece of toilet paper without it being soaked in water overnight. This made him quite useless as a guard dog, but the Queen used Furious because when he stood next to her, she looked even bigger than she was.

'My name is Ed, and I'm an old friend of Queenie's,' Ed said, trying to appear better friends with the Wide Witch than he truly was.

'"Queenie"?' the dog said. (At this point, Ed saw nothing remarkable about a talking animal. In fact, he found them rather annoying.) 'Yip! For such insolence – yap! – you must DIE!'

With this, the tiny dog leapt at Ed. Grabbing the turnup of his trousers between his tiny jaws, Furious began to worry it fiercely.

'Leave off!' Ed said crossly, for he had become attached to the outfit, outlandish as it was. He began hopping about, shaking his leg in an attempt to dislodge the fur-bearing bother.

Furious finally lost his grip, and Ed took this opportunity to put some distance between them. He ran around the large, gloomy hall, bumping into this and that. He finally clambered atop a table. Furious ran at him again and again, taking mighty leaps, but the table was too tall. Ed stood there, taunting the dog and enjoying its frustration.

A voice came from the end of the darkened hall. 'What's going on out here? That had *better* be the pizza guy.' It was the Wide Witch. She stood in utter darkness, save for a shaft of light coming from the open refrigerator into which she had been peering. In her right hand, she held an entire roast chicken, and was taking massive bites from it.

'Erm . . .' Ed paused. This wasn't quite the entrance he'd planned to make. 'I was just playing with your dog.'

'Don't listen to him – yip! – Your Majesty,' Furious said, out-of-breath. 'I'd never play with a – yap! Yap! – intruder.' The angry Yorkie shot Ed a dirty look.

'Stop your yapping, it's giving me a headache,' the Queen said, slamming the fridge door shut. 'You!' – she pointed at Ed – 'did you bring me any pizza?'

'Erm . . . no,' Ed said. 'Don't you remember? I'm the Son of—'

'Silence!' The Queen cut Ed off before the well-developed Rationalisation Lobe of his brain could really get going. Ed always resented this, as seat-of-the pants excuse-making made him feel really alive. Suddenly, he didn't like the Wide Witch much.

Furious bounded over to lick his mistress' toes. Ed took the opportunity to get down from the table. 'Yes, Snookums, I'm happy to see you too – if I *could* see you.'

(The Wide Witch hadn't seen her feet in a decade, at least; they were even whiter than the rest of her, from being in the shade.) 'Here you go.' She tossed a tidbit to Furious, who ate it with relish, then looked back at Ed as if to say, 'She likes me better than you.'

Ed didn't care. He was trying to figure out how to grab the Wide Witch's mammoth bird without getting too close to her mouth.

She was rummaging around inside the tables and cabinets tucked away in the hall. 'Furious, have you seen my special Son of Atom utensils? Boy, look in that drawer,' the Queen commanded.

Surely you grasped this coming eons ago, dear reader, but Ed Perversie was not as perceptive as you. Only now did it dawn on Ed exactly why the Queen was so interested in them, and his guts were gripped with fear. He was decently glad that his siblings hadn't made the trip. Ed looked in the drawer, and saw a fearsome set of ivory-handled implements.

'Nothing here,' he lied.

'Oh well,' the Queen said, tossing the chicken over her shoulder blithely. Furious scampered after it, and it was all Ed could do not to join him. 'I'll eat you peasant-style, fork and fingers.' Once again, she extracted her long golden fork from her voluminous robes. 'Where are the others? Hanging up somewhere dry-ageing perhaps? I know, you lose a lot of meat that way, but the flavour— mwah!' She smacked her lips.

As I'm sure you know, it is always offensive to be considered a comestible. Ed's spine stiffened, and outrage stimulated his morals. There would be no rationalisation this time; if I'm to be eaten, Ed thought, I hope the truth will make me less savoury. 'There are no others,' he said defiantly. 'Eat me if you like, but I saw through your secret plan from the beginning.'

'Secret?' the Queen said, moving into fork range. 'I thought I was pretty straightforward about it. After all, eating subjects at will is a Royal Prerogative.'

'_____!' This was the first time in Ed's life he'd ever used such strong language with an adult, and the boy felt a naughty power coursing through his body. He tensed to run.

Unfortunately the Queen saw this, and with a wave of her hand closed the great plywood doors to the hall. They slammed with a flimsy sound.

'Afraid so,' the Queen said. 'I know you're new here, but ignorance of the law is no excuse. Now,' she said. 'Be a good boy and flop on the ground a bit. You look like you need tenderizing.'

'No way, you awful lying _____!' Ed said. Unfortunately, the swearing buzz was a one-time thing. The immense woman rolled forward like a tidal wave of mayonnaise and raised her fork. Ed murmured a prayer. What could he do? She was still bigger than him, and since he was weak from hunger, probably just as fast. Then Ed got an idea: he'd try to take away her appetite.

'Asthma!' he shouted.

It worked! The Queen gave an inarticulate cry and recoiled. 'Where did you hear such foul language?'

Ed poured it on. 'Asthma! Asthma! Asthma!'

The Queen leapt on Ed, knocking him to the ground. 'Stop – saying – that!' she said, pummelling the boy. Furious danced around the struggling pair, barking insanely.

Ed struggled for all he was worth, but the masses of fake fur and fabric and flab made victory impossible. Soon, she had him pinned.

'Are you going to shut up and let me eat you, or am I going to have to eat you?' the Queen demanded.

'What kind of a choice is that?' Even though he was about to be eaten alive – and he didn't think she was cute any more, besides – being straddled by the Queen awakened certain feelings in Ed. That's how insane having a sex drive can be. I'm just telling you now, so you won't be surprised when you're an adult.

'You're right,' the Queen said, then looked thought-ful. 'I think I'll start with the ears.'

'Aiiiieeee!' Ed screamed as high as Sue used to, before the Professor's hormone treatments. He only had one chance at survival – he had to further the plot. 'Asthma is coming! They're all meeting him at the Stone Bathtub!'

It worked. The Queen pulled back from the boy's already saliva-drenched ear. 'Who told you that?'

'The beavers! I heard it at their house! That's where I came from tonight!'

'Oh, those two are nuts,' the Queen said. 'One of them hauls around pieces of wood like they're ch—'

Ed cut her off. 'I know! But what if they're right this time? A broken clock is right once a day.'

'Twice, actually.'

'Wait—' Ed said, trying figure that out, but his glucose-starved brain gave up almost immediately. 'Whatever. Can you afford to take the chance?'

The Queen sat up, then much to Ed's relief, stood up. 'You're right. I won't eat you – for the moment.' She clapped her hands, and bellowed out to unseen minions. 'Ready the sledge! And engage the Stealth Option.'

Excited by the volume of his mistress' voice, Furious Arf looked up from the shredded chicken and began yipping so frantically Ed thought he might be having a seizure. No such luck.

❖

Soon, Ed and the Queen were in the sledge. Both of them, and the dwarf driver, were covered by a heavy black blanket; this was the Stealth Option, and while it was always uncomfortable – scratchy and musty-smelling – with every minute the sky got brighter, and the more useless it became.

The Wide Witch began poking him with her fork, over and over, in various parts of his body. 'Ow . . . Ow . . . Ow!' Ed said. 'Why are you doing that?'

'Checking to see where you're the most tender,' the Witch said merrily. 'Plus, it's fun!'

What a mean person, Ed thought. For the first time in his life – but sadly, far from the last – some part of the boy was horrified that he had once liked someone so awful. 'What's the difference between a "sledge" and a "sled"?' he asked.

The Queen was entering her daily caloric intake into a small notebook. Such extravagant gluttony took tremendous discipline, and the Queen prided herself on maintaining a strict regimen of one-hundred-thousand calories per twenty-four hours.

'Listen,' she said crossly (for she had realised how far behind she was that day) 'just because I didn't eat you back there, that doesn't mean you can ask me annoying questions.' She turned away, then turned back. 'And I *will* eat you, I'm just saving you for dessert.'

Before Ed could respond, the sledge hit a muddy spot. One of the runners stuck, just for a moment – but the sledge was so heavy, and had been travelling at such a speed, that the sudden stop hurled the driver high into the air. The dwarf hit the ground with a sickening crunch.

'Stop fooling about!' the Wide Witch shouted. 'You only made that sound for sympathy.'

'Eff off, Your Majesty,' the dwarf groaned woozily, gingerly checking all his internal organs.

'What did you say?' the royal lard-dollop shouted, but the dwarf had momentarily blacked out. Meanwhile, several of the reindeer had unhooked themselves (because they were special, just as the Queen's driver had insisted) and were now clustered around their fallen leader. They drooled on him, hoping to wake him up.

A pint of spittle later, it worked. 'Ooh,' the dwarf said. 'I think I landed on my keys.'

'See, this is why we need workman's comp,' one reindeer said to the others. (Of course, to the dwarf and the Queen and Ed, this only sounded like a random series of snorts and whinnies.) 'This could be any one of us.' The reindeer, a big buck named Leathernose, raised a hoof and pointed to another. 'What if you got hurt, Puny Antlers? Do you think *she* would do anything about it?'

'No!' 'Not her!' came the answers.

'You – Buttsniffer – who's going to take care of your kids if, God forbid, we go off a glacier or something?'

'We'd just land in the snow,' Buttsniffer said.

'Wake up!' Leathernose said. 'The snow is melting! Anyway, that's not the point. The point is, do you think she'd send a helicopter to airlift us to the hospital?'

'Never!'

'Are you kidding?'

'What's a helicopter?'

'What's a hospital?'

'Can anybody see if there's a tick on my bum?'

Within moments, the Queen's reindeer had declared themselves an autonomous collective and, after a quick vote, wandered off into the forest.

Still dazed, the dwarf had remounted the sledge. He was set to give the reins a crack and hope for the best when the Witch yelled, 'Halt!'

'What is it now?' the dwarf said, turning around. 'I put the new bumper-sticker on before we left.'[19]

'That's not what I'm wondering about, you fool,' the

---

[19] On instructions from his sovereign, the dwarf had covered the rear panel of the sledge with sayings, things like 'If You Can Read This, Prepare to Become Icing,' 'Practise Random Acts of Cruelty,' and 'I Brake for Thinly Veiled Allegories.'

Witch said. 'Why did we stick back there? Could the snow be melting?' The Wide Witch oozed from the sledge and began measuring the local snowdrifts with her fork. Sure enough, they were dwindling.

This show of climatic defiance caused the always moody monarch to become unglued. The Wide Witch began running around the clearing, shaking her fist at the snow. 'I forbid you to melt!' she cried. 'If I wasn't weak from hunger . . . I need a snack.' Somewhat dispirited, she trudged back to the sledge, where Ed was wolfing down a chocolate bar he'd found mashed under the floormat. When he saw the Queen walking his way, he shoved the entire bar into his mouth. Eyes watering and cheeks painfully distended, Ed tried to breathe through his nose and hoped it would soften before he choked.

'You! What are you eating?'

'Nothing,' Ed attempted to say, but his mouth was too full, so he sucked some nougat into his lungs.

'That's all right,' the Queen said as Ed coughed violently. 'You're going to need your strength. Get down from there and hook yourself up. You're pulling the sledge.'

CHAPTER 10

 Discovering that one of your guests has sneaked away tends to take the mickey out of a party, and that is why all the etiquette books forbid it. Dinner with the beavers was no exception. After a brief circuit of the premises had proved beyond any doubt that Ed was gone, the beavers decided to flee.

'He'll bring the Wide Witch back with him, for sure,' Ruth rasped.

'We wouldn't want to be here when the Wide Witch arrives,' Naomi said. 'She's incredibly tedious.'

'Really?' Sue asked. She had been ostracised as a girl for the very same reason, and was loathe to judge someone else unfairly. 'Perhaps it simply takes a bit to get to know her.'

'Oh, we *know* her,' Naomi said.

'Yes, know and *hate* her.' Ruth turned to her mate. 'Do you remember those nasty brochures she used to hand out, the ones begging animals to turn evil? Carpeted the forest, she did – and the nasty things she said about Woody and Chip . . .'

'Speaking of the boys, why don't you get them ready for the trip to see Asthma?'

The magic name seemed to be causing less of an effect, thank goodness, or perhaps the children's stomachs were simply too empty to complain. Ruth hurried off, and presently the Perversies heard a litany of hyper-annoying babytalk coming from the other room. Minutes passed. Sue and Pete occupied themselves with a game of full-contact 'paper-scissors-stone' (the loser got punched). Loo ran around the room in circles until she got dizzy and collapsed, bonking her head.

Naomi grew impatient. 'We haven't a moment to lose,' she said. 'Honey, are you almost ready?'

'Just a second,' Ruth said. 'I'm nursing the boys.'[20]

More minutes passed. Their game over, Pete sat idly breaking small objects, while Sue busied herself slapping pointy things out of Loo's hands. Loo's instincts were unerring; see pointy thing, grab pointy thing, swoop pointy thing directly towards eye. Sue had to be on the top of her game, especially when her little sister crossed things up by switching to the earward route to her brain instead.

---

[20] This operation, which the children were exceedingly happy not to witness, was accomplished thanks to a small hole Naomi had drilled into each log with an auger.

'Honey . . .' Naomi said.

'I'm going as fast as I can. I'm letting them pick out their favourite outfits.'

'Oh for the love of God,' Naomi said. 'What's the point, if the Wide Witch eats us all?'

Ruth came out of the bedroom, with the logs tucked into a two-seat stroller, cleverly carved from wood. 'Fine, fine, keep your fur on,' she said. 'How many times do you think they'll meet Asthma in their lives? I want them to look nice, is that so much to ask?'

Naomi led Ruth, Woody, Chip, and the Perversie children out of the hut and into the moonlight.

'Doesn't seem as cold as it was,' Loo said.

'That'd be global warming,' Sue said, in a know-it-all tone. A split-second later, a snowball hit her on the side of the head.

'This packs GREAT!' Pete said. 'I wish Ed was here, so I could rub his face in it!' Under normal conditions, Pete's attack on Sue would've signalled a general melee. But it wasn't the same without Ed to gang up on, and frankly, they were too weak from hunger to do anything but trudge forward mindlessly.

Loo was sucking on a pine cone. 'Try it,' she said, offering the spit-covered cone to her sister.

Sue refused – only proper food passed her lips, thank

you very much – but Pete was game for anything, mostly because he lacked the higher mental functionality to discern the difference. Just as he was about to bite into the cone, Naomi said, 'This is the place.'

'What is the place?' Sue said.

'Our summer home,' Ruth said. 'It's hidden.'

'I wonder if the blue jays have been picking up our mail,' Naomi said.

'Here we go again,' Pete said, tossing the pine cone aside, and looking about for something hard enough to give him a concussion.

'What's his problem?' Naomi said, as Pete whacked his noggin against various objects.

'Long story,' Loo said. 'You'd have to be reading the book.'

'Oh.' Naomi removed some strategically placed evergreen boughs, revealing a hole.

'A hole?' Sue sniffed. 'I don't think so.'

'Come on, come on,' Naomi said, struggling with the stroller then handing it to her mate, who had already entered. 'Survival isn't for the squeamish. We'll be safe in here until morning.'

Loo, who had always wanted to be buried alive, scrambled inside with glee. A sudden gust of sleet, or perhaps just melting snow blown off the trees, convinced Sue that even a hole in the ground was better than standing outside all night. And so, after a quick pee, everyone clambered into the hole.

It was a tight fit, a jumble of unwanted arms and legs. 'Pete, if that's your hand—' Sue warned. Pete denied it, a smile in his voice.

Sue punched in the direction of the voice. She missed, hitting a thick root. 'Bugger!' she yelled, which is a very rude thing to say, especially in front of another species. Loo giggled at the profanity.

In addition to being a groper's paradise, the hole smelled awful. There was a powerful scent of wet fur, and it soon became clear that undigested cellulose gives humans terrible gas. On the plus side, however, Loo had found some wood lice and was eating them.

'Hey, don't bogart the vermin,' Pete said, scooping a handful.

Thanks to a lack of oxygen, everyone in the hole eventually drifted off into an uncomfortable slumber. As they slept, water trickled into the entrance from the melting world outside – and so by morning, the humans, beavers, and wooden proxy-children were laying in at least an inch of gelid mud.

Sue had woken up at first light. This was a lucky thing, for as soon as the puddle collecting on the hole's floor became deep enough, the sleeping Loo rolled over and attempted to bury her nose in it to drown herself. Grabbing Loo's hair, Sue yanked her little sister back from the Beyond again and again. Every time Sue did so, Loo rolled back into the puddle, eager to get an autograph from the Grim Reaper.

Amazing, Sue thought. Loo wasn't even *awake*. Sue brushed someone's slightly poop-scented back paw away from her face, and began wondering how being back with the Professor could possibly be any worse than this. Suddenly, she heard a noise outside. It sounded like slurred singing, punctuated by belching, and bells.

Like a flash, Naomi popped out of the hole. Sue saw her dart out into the weak morning light. The bells got louder, and Sue hissed, 'What is it?'

'Stay back,' Naomi said, as the others started to stir.

'Do you need help?' Ruth whispered to Naomi, clambering over the others towards the front of the hole. 'I'm coming.' She stepped on Pete's face, giving him a muddy paw-print on his cheek. 'Naomi?' Naomi didn't answer.

Not knowing what was about to happen, Ruth pressed Woody and Chip, in mud-sodden swaddling clothes, into Sue's unwilling arms. 'You seem the . . . well, *least irresponsible*,' Ruth said. 'Make sure they get to Asthma. If this front entrance becomes blocked, dig your way out with your powerful front claws.'

'But I don't have —'

It was too late; Ruth had already scrambled out of the hole after her mate.

Pete was now awake enough to push his siblings around. 'Move,' he said. 'I want to see.'

'Suits me,' Sue said, moving towards the back. To Loo she said, 'There's the back wall. Start digging.'

'Goody!' Loo said, hoping for a cave-in.

Pete saw the two beavers crouched in the path of a grimy man dressed in red. The man had a sack over his shoulder, which was dripping fluid of some kind. It clinked merrily with every step the man took; less merry, to be sure, was the stench that seemed to come off the man like steam from a cup of hot tea. (Pete's nose suggested that hot urine might be more appropriate.) The man had a florid face, an unkempt beard and a booming, inappropriate laugh that frequently deteriorated into a hacking cough. 'Ho, ho, ho . . .' the man mumbled to himself. Then, somewhat bitterly: 'HA!'

Could it be? Pete thought. After all this time, did *Father Xmas* really exist? Pete stopped himself – what a thought for someone nearly thirteen years old! There was no Father Xmas. This fellow was merely a

The Chronicles of Blarnia

semi-continent layabout who had parleyed people's love of Christmas into a swindle. He wished Ed were here – it takes a con artist to catch a con artist. The wind changed direction, and Pete's eyes watered a bit from the scent of body odour and rotgut liquor. Still, the man sure *looked* like Father Xmas . . .

The man took a slug from a bottle of spiked nog cleverly hidden inside a greasy paper bag. Every ten feet or so, a reindeer would scamper out of the tree line and jam its red, lit-up nose into the man's rear end, giving it a good buzz. Pete saw the man turn and swipe blindly. He stumbled, nearly fell, then uttered a string of profanities unheard outside of several now-disbanded branches of the armed forces.

'Nice language, Father Xmas,' Naomi said.

The spirit stopped in his tracks, and looked down at the beavers.

'Hm. Wombats,' he said, scratching himself. 'So now it's talking wombats, is it? Want to play rough, eh Mr Brain? I'll fix you soon enough.' Father Xmas threw the nog away, and slung the pack down on the ground. He opened it and began fishing around. 'You're just a figment of my imagination. Yesterday, it was copulating barley twists,' he mumbled. 'After I drink this new booze, wombats, you're going to disappear . . .' He continued pawing through the pack which was apparently filled with broken and leaking containers of the hard stuff. 'C'mon, gimme a winner. I'm sick of gin-nog. Hey, wombats,' Father Xmas said.

'We're beavers,' Ruth said.

Father Xmas paid no attention. 'Do you know my secret recipe for gin-nog? Instead of eggs, you put gin in it.' The jolly old elf gave a wink. 'You can also substitute gin for the nog part, too.' He pulled a festive-looking bottle out of the pack, stood up, then took a drink. 'Blech, cranberry liqueur.' He made a face. 'Seasonally appropriate, but just as revolting as ever. Want some? "Lil holiday spirit?' He cackled at the pun.

'No thanks, I never drink before eight a.m.,' Naomi said sardonically.

'Suit yourself. 'Course, it could be worse. It could be some of Mrs Claus' homemade mistletoe brandy. That stuff'll kill you in small doses, for sure . . . but if you drink enough of it very *quickly* – you want it to turn on itself, y'see . . .' The reindeer swooped in from behind. 'Arrgh!' the spirit howled incoherently. 'Rudolph, you son of a – just try that one more time and I'll—' He hawked up a sugarplum-sized glob of mucus and spat it at the reindeer. It missed by a mile.

Watching this unfold, Pete's mouth hung open so long that his tongue was rimed with frost. It *was* Father Xmas – and not the wholesome spirit of earlier years, before the Queen had banished the holiday. A hundred years of unemployment had turned Father Xmas into a vast, hairy marshmallow rolled in stink. Once fair, hardworking, and beloved by all, now Father Xmas embodied all the worst aspects of the holiday – the easy gluttony and conniving, the craven self-interest cloaked in false heartiness. Even the ever-expanding nature of the season ('. . . only a hundred shopping days left before Christmas!') had taken up residence in Father Xmas; his largeness was no longer an exuberant abundance of person, it was the grey, heart-straining flab caused by a diet of fruitcake and mini candy-canes, topped off with little physical activity other than masturbation.

The spirit now teetered in front of the beavers. Naomi had her arms folded and wore a disapproving expression. 'We've been wondering what happened to you.'

'Actually, not,' Ruth added acidly.

'What happened to your reindeer?' Naomi asked.

'Repossessed,' Father Xmas said. 'Except for the mutant.' He turned and shouted into the forest, 'Yeah, Rudy, I called you a mutant! What do you think of *that*?'

Ruth clucked her tongue. 'And your sleigh is up on blocks in the front garden, am I right?'

'Don't take that tone with me,' the spirit slurred. 'I'm Father Xmas, goddammit!'

'You better not let Asthma hear you talking like that,' Naomi said.

'Asthma can go—!' He reared back, as if to kick the much smaller beavers. They scattered. 'That's right, *run*! Run for your lives . . . Stupid wombats . . . Varmints . . .'

'Too slow, St. Dickolas,' Ruth said saltily, from a safe distance.

'Yeah,' Naomi added. 'Nice nog tits!'

Father Xmas said something much too rude to be repeated in this book, even with CensorVision. The beavers laughed, just out of reach.

'Did you know that a stocking with coal in it is the perfect weapon?' Father Xmas bellowed menacingly, his breath billowing out in great, alcoholic clouds. 'Leaves no marks. Totally untraceable. And I *can* climb down your chimney . . .'

That threat had teeth, and the beavers stopped teasing the spirit. 'Seriously, Asthma's on the move,' Naomi said. 'He's back.'

'Ahhh, he's been saying that for years,' Father Xmas said bitterly. He took a dispirited swig. 'Maybe he should've come back before this place turned into a no-Christmas hellhole.'

'You better pull yourself together, man,' Ruth said. 'Christmas isn't just your job. It's Asthma's birthday, and he won't appreciate you acting so sloppy. We're going to see him right now, and the first thing we're going to say is —'

'I remind you, talking wombat, that I know when you are sleeping, and I know when you're awake. I know if you've been bad or good, so —'

'Your files don't scare us,' Naomi said. 'Anyway, you're one to talk about being naughty.' Father Xmas also embodied the part of Christmas that makes people get wasted at office parties and have clumsy, cramp-inducing sex with co-workers in broom closets. He'd embodied that a lot lately.

Maybe it was true contrition, or maybe simply the ever-shifting moods of the sodden, but Father Xmas' tone changed abruptly 'Really? Asthma's really back? I'm sure he'll understand – he loves to forgive things.' Then the spirit's mood changed again, this time to self-pity. 'Not my fault I got sacked,' he said. 'No Christmas – what am I supposed to do, become Father Tax-Preparation Day?'

'Makes more sense than stumbling around the forest drunk out of your mind,' Naomi said.

'Does it?' Father Xmas said with a last flicker of belligerence. 'I don't think so. Whoop.' He fell down, then began to blubber. 'All the sodding animals call me "Father Ex-mas" . . . I've wasted my life. I'm immortal and I've wasted my life.'

'Did you talk to that friend of ours,' Ruth asked, 'the one who wanted you to be a process-server?'[21]

'Nah, I didn't feel like it,' Father Xmas said.

Back at the entrance to the hole, Pete suddenly saw the usefulness of myths. Meanwhile, Loo had wormed her way next to him.

'Is that . . . Father Xmas?' she asked, voice filled with wonder.

Pete didn't know what to say. Loo had always had an extreme – some might say unhealthy – attachment to Christmas. Every year when her school put on its Nativity play, she had insisted on playing Baby Jesus, even after she had grown so large that her legs dangled from the crib quite absurdly. Christmas was Loo's favourite holiday, not least because she always seemed

[21] As you doubtless know, dear reader, a process-server is someone who delivers a letter notifying you that someone is suing you, someone like the author of something you've parodied for example. Under normal circumstances, people do everything they can to avoid this person, but if they saw Father Xmas coming up the road, naturally they'd expect a present. By the time they realised that he was giving them legal documents, it would be too late. It was an excellent idea, one sure to succeed.

to find sharp little toys to choke on in her Christmas pudding. Ed delighted in hiding other things in her pudding, unsavoury things like a pickled half-dissected frog, or the sweat-stained tongue from a ratty old trainer. Pete knew that Ed had been devising more and more elaborate ways to prove to Loo once and for all that Father Xmas didn't exist. So far, she had always stood firm, but this . . . finding out Father Xmas was a smelly old drunk would destroy her.

'No,' Pete said, 'it's just some wandering—' He didn't want to say "drunk" in front of Loo. '—minstrel.'

'No it's not,' she told her brother indignantly. 'You know what Mum says, "When you lie about Christmas, Baby Jesus spits up."' She turned back. 'Sue,' Loo called, 'come see Father Xmas.'

'You have to understand,' Father Xmas said to the beavers. 'Tell Asthma: once Christmas was cancelled, there was nothing left for me to do – nothing left but to sit and think,' Father Xmas said.

'*Drink*, you mean,' Ruth said.

'Don't mind if I do.' He tipped back the bottle, then finding it empty, tossed it into the bushes. 'Uh-oh. My pack's getting light, and Blarnia sober is no place I want to be. If you'll excuse me, I have to be getting back to my cave full of booze – old presents. It took years for people to get out of the habit, even after the holiday was cancelled.'

'Well, it's un-cancelled, so I'd start drinking black coffee pronto,' Ruth said.

'Great,' Father Xmas said sourly.

'I thought you would be happy,' Naomi said.

'Oh yeah, I'm overjoyed,' he said sarcastically. 'Who wouldn't want to be on the phone all night? "Yes, it's on again, no, I don't know why, it's not my problem you can't fit into your costume any more . . ." '

'On the phone?' Ruth rasped. 'To whom?'

'Santa Claus, Papa Noel, Strega Buffana, Helliger Nikolaus, Kerstman, the little dwarf Jultomten, Father Frost, Snowflake Girl – I'd sure love to have her melt all over me, woaagghh . . .'

At Father Xmas' disgusting groan of lust, the beavers looked at each other. Ruth was the first to speak. 'You're making all those people up!'

'No, I'm not. Wish I were,' Father Xmas said. 'I'm stuck with you lot, but Christmas is everywhere. America, Mexico, France, Italy, Norway . . . everybody's got their Christmas spirit. Or did you think only English people celebrated Christmas?' Father Xmas sniffed. 'Bigot.'

'Wino,' Ruth spat back. It was getting ugly.

'I prefer "gin-o," ' Father Xmas said.

Back at the hole, Loo was trained on Father Xmas like a cat stalking a mouse. 'He looks drunk,' Loo said, then with alarm, 'I think he's leaving!' Now Pete saw something quite terrifying – he saw the usually pleasant-if-vacant features of his little sister transform themselves into a Kabuki mask of pure greed.

'Father Xmas!' Loo screamed. 'Over here! Father Xmas, *I want a present!*' Climbing out of the hole, Loo galloped through the muddy snow towards the group, screeching 'Gimme! Gimme! Gimme!' Before she had covered the twenty feet, the words had devolved into something deeply disturbing, a guttural chant of avarice.

Though Pete didn't see this, preferring sport to anthropology, there was something primal in Loo's behaviour, something that harkened back to our species' earliest days . . . with young ape-humans concealed in the trees, or hunkered down behind tufts of grass, waiting for the 'gift' of a sick antelope or straggling, befuddled wildebeest. The hunger was terrifying. Father Xmas knew this look well; even in the good old days, it had haunted his dreams. When he saw the child, Father Xmas turned and ran. Unfortunately, between his impaired balance and the slickness of his bootsoles, he sprawled almost immediately.

Loo leapt on him, ignoring the body odour that came off him in waves. 'I wanna present!' she cried. Loo's mad dash had caused a stampede; Pete and Sue bolted out of the hole, galvanised by the possibility of getting something for nothing.

'Help! Help!' Father Xmas yelped, as he struggled against the little girl. He looked over at Ruth and Naomi. 'I'm sorry I called you "varmints"! Get her off me!'

'Sorry,' Ruth said, her stubby arms folded. 'It's time for you to be Father Xmas again. The snow is melting.'

'I thought there was something wrong with my eyes . . . Get off me, kid.' He struggled to his feet, shaking Loo off. Whenever he did, she sprang back, and grabbed him again.

'Oh, no you don't,' she said. 'I'm not letting you go until you give me a present! Did you get the letter I sent you? Did you, huh? Did you?' Loo babbled.

'Sock 'im in the goolies,' Pete yelled, laughing. 'That oughta get you something!'

'Okay, I've got something for you,' Father Xmas said wearily. 'I've got presents for all of you.' He began turning out his pockets, then started rummaging in his soiled and dripping sack.

'I don't think I want anything if it comes from there,' Loo said, pointing.

Father Xmas gave her a look that could've warmed the North Pole. 'Shut up! You'll take what I give you and like it. Honest to God, it's kids like you that make my life such a hell!' He turned to the beavers. 'Do you understand, wombats? Do you understand *now* why I drink?'

'Beavers,' Ruth corrected.

'Don't waste your breath,' Naomi said. 'He probably won't even remember this tomorrow.'

Father Xmas dug around in his pack, Loo began circling him like a shark. She began a rhythmic back-arching that oceanographers call 'attack posture.' Just as she was about to head in for the kill, Father Xmas extracted a small bottle, about the size and shape of aeroplane booze.

'D'you really think that's appropriate?' Ruth scolded. 'What is she, eight?'

'It's not that,' Father Xmas said, as Loo fairly snatched it out of his hand. She had it uncorked and halfway to her mouth before she asked, 'Is it poisonous?'

'Nope. Not even if you drink the whole bottle,' Father Xmas said. 'Now available without a prescription, it's a precious ointment to be used only in the greatest emergencies.'

Pete saw the look on Loo's face and asked, 'If you don't want it, give it to me – I'd like to see how far I could chuck it.'

Loo considered for a second, then put it into her

pocket. 'That's okay,' she said. Maybe Professor Berke could analyse it, and tell her if it had any dangerous interactions. It was worth a shot.

Now Sue chimed in. 'Loo,' she said, 'if it isn't poisonous, maybe we can eat it.'

'No! It's my present, and I won't share it!'

Father Xmas fished something out of his pack and gave it to Pete. 'Here.' It was a small bone.

'THANK CHRIST!' Pete exclaimed. Deliriously happy, he bit into it – and spat it out. 'It's rubber!'

'Of course,' Father Xmas said.

'It looks used,' Sue said.

'Maybe it is,' Father Xmas said. 'I forget where I got it. It's a chew toy.'

'Why in the world would I want a bloody chew toy?' Pete said, making to throw it. To him, the world was divided into two categories: things you could throw, and things you were going to throw, just hadn't figured out how yet.

Sue held his arm. 'Don't,' she said. 'Remember, we're in a book. We might need it.'

'Wise girl,' Father Xmas said. 'Here's yours. I got it in New Orleans.'

Sue looked at the shiny green object; it was a cone of soiled paper reading 'Happy Mardi Gras,' a cheap noisemaker. There was lipstick on the white plastic mouthpiece. Wiping it off with disgust, Sue blew a quiet note, then made a face. 'Tastes like cigarettes,' she said.

Pete laughed. 'At least my thing can't give me herpes,' he said meanly.

'At least my thing can't give me rabies,' Sue snapped back.

The morning was beautiful, the sunrise lighting every dropping drip and running rivulet like golden diamonds. Too bad the company was so poor.

They were walking single-file through the forest at a good clip, with the beavers in the lead. The Perversie children straggled behind, bickering and bending back evergreen branches and whopping each other with them. The beavers had long since given up trying to keep the children quiet, but had found that with a little practice, the constant stream of teasing and tears laced with mild profanities could be tuned out successfully.

'Since when did Father Xmas get *sarcastic*?' Ruth said.

'Watch out for this hole, it's an ankle-twister,' Naomi said, stepping over it. 'He's a terrible alcoholic, dear. Did you see his face? "Cheeks like roses"? "Nose like a cherry"? Couldn't be more obvious.'

Ruth shook her head sadly. 'That's just not right.'

They walked on in silence for a bit. Just as Loo gave a yelp – she had twisted her ankle – Ruth said to Naomi, 'I really think we should consider becoming Jewish.'

CHAPTER 11

Everyone else in Blarnia might have been overjoyed about winter's easing at last, but as he attempted to yank the heavily laden sledge through an ever-deepening quagmire, Ed was unenthusiastic.

'This Stealth Option is useless!' the Wide Witch cried, throwing back the heavy blanket.

'*Your* idea,' the dwarf said quietly.

'Did you say something?' the Witch asked irritably.

'Oh, no, Your Travesty.'

The Witch did a double-take, then continued. 'It's bloody stifling under there. I feel like I'm buried alive!'

'If only,' the dwarf mumbled.

'I didn't catch that,' the Wide Witch said.

'I said, "As you wish," Your Majesty,' the dwarf said.

'No you didn't,' the Witch said.

The dwarf didn't like where this was going, so he lashed Ed a bit. This always made the Witch laugh. But even the best jokes get played out eventually, so the dwarf attempted to engage Her Jiggliness in a discussion of meteorology.

'So, like, how did you do it?' the dwarf asked, looking back over his shoulder. 'Did you command the same weather system to remain over us for a whole century?'

The Witch examined her cuticles in the weak morning light, profoundly uninterested. 'Yeah, I think so. I never really thought about it.'

'But then, if there was always snow, but never any melting, wouldn't we eventually get buried? How did you keep the snow down to a manageable level? And what about the territories around Blarnia? Surely their weather got all bollocksed up as a result, tornadoes and such at the very least? And the trees and animals – how did they survive? I think,' the dwarf said, with an air of intellectual triumph, 'I think we've all been in suspended animation!'

The Witch looked up from her increasingly frantic search for a massive ziplock bag full of tapioca she'd packed for the journey. 'Oh shut up, will you?' she barked, irritated about the missing food. 'It was magic, you dimwit! I just said a few words, waved my wand, and shazam, it was Winter.' To the Witch, science was all so much mumbo-jumbo, which people too softheaded to do magic retreated to whenever they wanted to explain an inconvenient reality.

'But—'

'Silen!' the Witch shouted through a full mouth. 'Ah'm eatie mah pudda!' There was much slurping and smacking of lips.

Frightened to look behind him, the dwarf clammed up. His hair was blown forward by a mighty belch, and for a while the only sound was the drip and trickle of melting snow, liberally punctuated by Ed's grunting and complaints.

'But why winter?' the dwarf finally said.

'It goes better with my colouring,' the Witch said, licking her spoon, in a better mood now that she'd had a little something to eat. She took off her outermost wrap, and fanned herself. The winter was ending, but The Sweating had just begun.

Spitting out the bit, Ed stopped. 'Memo to self,' Ed wheezed into his finger. 'Must rest.' Never brawny under the best of circumstances, pulling the sledge through the thickening muck was proving to be more than he could bear. Legs giving out, he dropped down, smearing his satin Sergeant Pepper jacket with freezing mud.

Dozing in the back, the Wide Witch was jolted awake by the stopping of the sledge. She sat up, rod-straight, and bellowed, 'WHA-AT? You DARE to stop?' She halted mid-rant; her attention had been caught by some tiny shrieking and giggling that had emanated from the base of a tree to their left. All the occupants of the sledge looked down.

There, much to everyone's amazement, some denizens of the forest were engaged in a holiday office party. There was a family of squirrels, a satyr, a dwarf and an old dog-fox, all as merry as a bit of time off and plenty of Father Xmas-donated alcohol could make them. Generally they all disliked each other, especially the old dog-fox who was the boss, but Father Xmas had come through earlier dispensing social lubricant, and so a fragile conviviality was being observed. Christmas carols were being played by a small boombox, connected to an outlet in the tree. Someone had put food colouring in the watercooler. The shrieks and giggles were coming from the lady dwarf, who the satyr was attempting to convince to sit on the fax machine without any panties on.

'C'mon,' the satyr wheedled. 'It'll be great – we'll send it to the Home Office. They won't have any idea who it's from. You don't have any distinctive moles, do you?'

'Yeah, c'mon,' Ed added, totally absorbed by this vignette. He'd never seen a real, live naked female of any species, except for Loo when she was a baby, and that didn't count.

The Wide Witch stood in the sledge. No one paid

any attention. She cleared her throat. Still nothing. Finally, she put her fork to her lips and blew into the end, producing a blast of jagged sound. The party went silent, but only for the briefest moment.

An adult squirrel looked at a bottle in his hand. 'Jesus Christ, I think this crap is making me hear things.'

'Could be a brain tumour,' his wife said, then turned to one of her offspring. 'You've had enough,' she said, taking a biscuit from him and stuffing it into her mouth. 'Those are good,' she said, grabbing the plate and beginning to shovel.

'What's going on here?' the Wide Witch roared, doubly incensed at the affront of anyone eating anything but herself. 'What's the meaning of this?'

'It's her,' the old dog fox whispered out of the corner of his muzzle. '*La Strega Grossissima*. When I give the signal, everybody do what we practised . . . Ahem, ahem.' The old dog fox stood up unsteadily, clutching a bottle of beer in his hand. 'Just a bit of holiday fun,' he said, in a voice rather too loud to be strictly appropriate. 'I find it helps morale – we're not just a company, y'see, we're also a family.'

'I see,' the Wide Witch said, with menace in her voice. 'And where do I fit in the family?'

'Why, you're the CEO,' the dog-fox stammered.

Michael Gerber

'We've reached our quota for the quarter – we've been slaving day and night to fill a big order for treacly-talking-animal-style whimsy from China, and I simply thought everybody could use . . .'

A fresh gale of laughter came from the direction of the fax machine.

'QUIET!' the Witch yelled, then turned to the dwarf who, like Ed, was watching that situation with definite interest. She hit him. 'Remind me why I pay you? You've got a bloody whip! Use it!' The Witch turned back to the dog fox. 'And you – I should've expected this from you. You simply don't have the judgement necessary for a management position. First, you can't decide whether you're a dog or a fox, and now . . . this.'

'But Madame Chairman, it's not strictly my fault. As you can tell by all the empties'—the dog-fox gestured at the various piles of empty bottles strewn about – 'Father Xmas came by.'

'Father Xmas!' the Witch exclaimed.

'Do you know where he went?' the dwarf asked politely. 'He owes me some money.'

The Witch biffed him on the noggin. 'But that's impossible,' she said to the dog-fox. 'Surely this was a ridiculous hallucination.'

'So are you,' Ed muttered. The Witch didn't hear

him. He didn't care, he was happy for the rest. He sneaked a piece of fruitcake that was just within reach.

'It wasn't! It wasn't!' a small squirrel said.

'Shh!' his mother said, taking a biscuit from her plate and giving it to him so he would quiet down.

'Dear, don't do that,' her husband said. 'You'll give him an unhealthy relationship to food.'

The squirrel mother was beginning a long defence of her actions when the Witch hollered, 'Enough! All you idiots drive me crazy!' She raised her fork.

'Okay, everybody,' the dog-fox said. 'Go for it!' In the moment before they were all turned to statues of buttercream icing, the entire party whirled around and presented their bare bottoms to Her Highness.

The dwarf let out a snicker, which he quickly stifled. The Witch glared at him.

'Something caught in my throat,' the dwarf said.

'Being Queen wouldn't be half as bad, if you didn't have to put up with subjects,' the Queen muttered. Hearing this, the dwarf made a face of innocent fealty, but the Queen wasn't buying it. 'Don't think you're not included in that, my bucko! So' – she turned to Ed – 'ready to get back to work?'

'Are you kidding?' Ed said. He pointed to the runners of the sledge, which were now sunk deep into the melty muck. 'This thing isn't going anywhere.'

'Then we must walk,' the Witch said, getting out of the sledge.

Ed couldn't believe his ears. 'Wait a moment,' he said, taking the bridle off his face and whipping it into the woods. 'We're *walking*? Not much of a witch, are you?'

'I'd watch my tongue if I were you, boy,' the Witch fumed.

'Or what, you'll spank me? That's about all that wand is good for, apparently.'

Still perched atop the sledge, the dwarf was enraptured by Ed's insolence. He leaned over and buried his head in his hands, quaking silently with laughter.

The Wide Witch saw him. 'What's your problem?'

'Nothing,' the dwarf said with great effort. 'I'm just overcome with . . . fear. Fear of your awesome power. That's why I'm shaking.'

'And pray, what explains the laughter?'

The dwarf had to pause frequently, lest he lose control completely. 'It . . . isn't laughter . . . my Queen, I am crying . . . crying out of my very great fear.' As he said these last words, the dwarf had to jam his fist into his mouth and bite down on it until the blood came.

'Uh-huh.' The Witch wasn't convinced. 'Come down here and tie this boy up, so he doesn't run away.'

'Tie me up?' Ed snorted with disbelief. 'Don't you

know a binding spell or something? His nasty jerkin is more magical than you!' Ed said, pointing at the dwarf.

The dwarf looked down at his chest. 'It's not nasty,' he said, hurt. 'I got this at a Renaissance Fayre.'

The Witch didn't say anything, looking off into the middle distance as she finished off a tube of Pringles and thinking how much more rewarding and fun life would be if there were no subjects in it. Oh well – at least she'd been able to swipe some food from the forest office party, thought the Witch as she sucked back a bowlful of dip.

Meanwhile, the dwarf was trying to bind Ed's hands, but there was nothing available. Finally, he looped a liquorice bootstrap around Ed's wrists. 'Now, don't break that,' the dwarf commanded. 'Pretend it's steel cable.'

Ed broke it. 'Sorry, I'm really hungry,' he said, popping it into his mouth.

The Witch stormed over. Tearing the end off the empty crisp tube, she jammed one of Ed's hands into it. Before Ed could wriggle away, she jammed his other hand in there, too, and the boy was effectively handcuffed.

'There!' she said. 'Now, can we go?'

The threesome began to walk. Hunger and petulance meant that Ed brought up the rear.

'This sucks,' Ed said to no one in particular.

'Shut up and carry my fur,' the Witch said, slinging it over his shoulder. Lugging the tarpulin-sized pelt, the boy stumbled along looking daggers at the sweaty mound galumphing along querulously in front of him, her impossible buttocks giving an extra shake whenever she'd haul off and whack the dwarf. He wriggled his hands out of the tube, and tossed it aside. Ed wondered how he could've ever been attracted to such an ill-tempered, utterly repellent loser – and in that moment, not through any chronological marker, sexual experience or social triumph, Ed Perversie became an adult.

'Stop!' the Wide Witch cried, cocking a flab-ringed ear.

'What is it, Your Majesty?' the dwarf asked.

'Shh!' Suddenly, they became aware of the most curious sound – a sort of rushing, cracking, blowing, buzzing sound. It was faint, but growing louder.

'It's nothing,' the Witch said. 'I thought I heard an ice-cream truck.'

They began to walk again, and suddenly it was upon them. Blarnia was undergoing massive global warming – water levels leapt upwards from the run-off, as vast ice-shelves splintered explosively, sending icebergs the size of Liechtenstein careening off in all directions. A sizzling sirocco abruptly blew against Ed's face, pelting it with sand from the deserts spreading almost as fast as the water. A mosquito buzzed and bit, pumping Ed full of malaria and yellow fever. 'You should meet my little sister,' Ed said as his immune system crumpled.

'How odd,' the Wide Witch said, suddenly in ankle-deep water.

A squirrel dressed as a bird rocketed past the group; he was in a tiny kayak, riding the wee rapids that surrounded them. 'Yee-HAW!' the squirrel said.

'My Queen, I fear that this isn't a thaw,' the dwarf said. 'This is *spring*!'

'But it can't be!' the Witch said. 'If it's spring, that can only mean one thing . . .'

She and the dwarf exchanged a look of horror as they chorused: '. . . the end of the Financial Year!'

CHAPTER 12

'Are we there yet?' Loo whined.

While the Wide Witch feverishly wondered about how she was going to pay a century's worth of back taxes, the beavers drove the Perversie children ever onward through the forest. Up hill and down dale they went, bravely complaining and trying not to become alarmed about the rapidly shifting weather.

'No worries,' Pete said. 'The weather isn't really changing. It's just a bunch of tree-hugging alarmists armed with junk science.'

Sue – the only one of the group who knew, or indeed cared to know, anything about the seasons – was convinced that the Earth had fallen off its axis and was hurtling toward the Sun.

'Cool!' Loo said, then dropped to the ground and tried to give the planet a shove.

Impending planet-wide catastrophe tended to put their troubles into perspective, even the hunger that still gnawed at their bellies. Pete had begun to suck his belt for nourishment.

'You should try it,' he said to his sisters. 'It reminds me of food.' Loo chewed the fringe of her vest, but all it did was give her funny-tasting spit.

All around them birds sang and animals mated, going at it like, well, animals. And who could blame them? It had been a long, cold, and very lonely hundred years.

'What are those animals doing?' Loo asked her sister, pointing at a pair of amorous woodchucks.

'Erm . . .' Sue stalled. 'Playing.'

'Really?' Loo said. 'One of them's screaming.'

'Rent a room!' Naomi shouted.

'Keep your eyes on the path,' Sue said, 'or else you'll lose your other shoe.'

'I lost my sock, too,' Loo said.

Crossing a forest in full rut wasn't the only less-than-pleasant aspect of the journey. The smell that hung around them was incredible, especially in the low areas, where a nasty all-natural stew had collected. Unlocked by the new warmth, tons of once-frozen vegetable matter began to rot enthusiastically. All around them, one hundred years of decay was being compressed into the space of a few hours; millions of maggots and lice jostled underfoot, and the air was nearly unbreathable with the sweet stench of putrefaction.

'I know it's part of nature,' Ruth said, 'but I wish it could've held out at least until we'd got to Asthma's.'

'Not far now,' Naomi said.

An hour later Loo asked, 'Are we there yet?' and they paused for a small celebration commemorating the ten-thousandth time she had uttered that phrase. Of course by 'celebration' I mean 'five short, sharp swats on the bottom.'

Just when the children thought they couldn't walk any further – or at least when the author had gotten good and tired of describing them doing so – they walked up a hill, and there it was, a green, open crown of turf that looked over the forest like a lord. There was no fetid muck or sex-crazed squishy-noise-making animals up here, only bright sun, and a clean, salt-tinged breeze coming in from the sea. Some distance away, there was a massive, rectangular object. It looked to be immensely aged, hewn from the living rock, and covered with graffiti of some kind.

'That's the Stone Bathtub,' Naomi said in a hushed tone.

Loo, who spurned the touch of soapy water, felt a tickle of dread. 'What's that?' she asked, pointing at a large beige tent. As its pennants snapped in the steady breeze, they saw that 'Welcome Stutts Class of 1952' had been crossed out and 'Welcome Asthma!' not so neatly substituted.

'Yeah,' Sue added. 'What's that mean?' But before

either beaver had time to answer, Pete had smelled something.

'Food!' he cried, and sprinted towards the pavilion. Sue and Loo followed, fast on his heels.

The crowd of chatting animals milling under the tent spied the Perversies sprinting towards them and wisely cleared a path to the all-you-can-eat buffet. The children hit the steam table at full gallop, and began stuffing food down their throats. Pete was so hungry that he swallowed a discarded bottle cap.

Under the pavilion was also a bar, with a satyr mixing drinks.

'You know, I was as sick of the cold as the next talking animal,' a wolverine squatting there said, 'but it certainly did keep the smell down.'

'I'm glad we're high up!' The great horned owl next to him laughed, then asked conspiratorially, 'Do you reckon the rumours were true? About the bears having an orgy instead of hibernating?'

'Couldn't say,' the wolverine said, 'wasn't invited. But I wouldn't put it past them.' He looked over at the Perversie children, digging massive handfuls of food out of the steam-trays and dumping it into their mouths. 'Get a load of the hairless apes.'

Under the tent there was all manner of delicious food – slightly grayish ham, well picked-over roast beef, charred ends of potatoes, sausages that had spent all day swimming in tepid grease, cold porridge that someone had put their cigarette out in. Okay, so perhaps it wasn't such delicious food, but hunger covers a multitude of flaws, and so the children were tucking in like the savages they were. Not surprisingly, Loo began to choke.

The owl put down his tumbler of Scotch and toddled over to the girl. As she went dangerously lavender, he took up position behind Loo to brace her, and the wolverine sprinted full speed in her direction. The furry Good Samaritan butted Loo right in the stomach, and several pounds of impacted lasagna untouched by human tooth sprayed on to the grass.

'Mff-ff,' Sue said, and Pete concurred.

'Don't mention it,' the animals chorused.

'Want to go and see whether the Asthma Arse-Kissing Society has thinned out a bit?' the wolverine asked.

'Lead on,' the owl said.

Asthma stood in the centre of a vast, pulsing mass of creatures. There were unicorns and unitards, and a bull with the head of a fly, and dryads and nyads and nomads and olympiads. There were chimpäera and realtaurs and even a sphinxter or two.

But Asthma himself – you never would've guessed he

was worth all this fuss, just by looking at him. He was merely a black house cat; an exceedingly furry one, to be sure, with big greenish-yellow eyes, but nothing impressive at all. The cat's coat (which he groomed incessantly) was so thick that from the rear he seemed to be wearing a pair of dark-grey bloomers. And his ridiculously poofy tail, which was invariably up, hung like a cloud of smoke over him. Asthma wasn't a purebred – in fact, there were clearly so many different kinds of cat contained within him that he was slightly awkward-looking. He was even somewhat on the small-ish side. And yet, they all stood around him, trying to win his favour. For Asthma himself saw nothing wrong with his appearance – and this comfort in his own fur gave him a dignity that commanded respect. (Also it was rumoured that he had super-powers.) Two caramel-dappled gerbils played around Asthma's feet, and teased him about the tufts of black fur that stuck out comically between his toes.

'Watch it, or I might eat you,' Asthma joked. The gerbils scattered, giggling.

'Asthma! Asthma!' the crowd of animals cried, each one jockeying for his attention, each one determined to show that he was more devoted than the animal next to them. Brief fisticuffs broke out between a marmot and a fiddler crab and had to be broken up by an ocelot.

Then, a female fairy penguin threatened to kill herself if Asthma wouldn't be with her for ever.

'But I am with you,' Asthma pointed out.

'Oh,' the fairy penguin said, and stumbled off in search of another reason to be depressed and dramatic.

It was a wild scene, as all the denizens of Blarnia brave enough to defy the Wide Witch threw their lot in with the new boss. Some hoped that he would help them become rich and powerful, or help them vanquish their enemies. Others had 'once-in-a-lifetime' investment opportunities or business deals that they wanted Asthma to join.

'Look, Asthma,' a pterodon said. 'It's a hat, but it's also an umbrella!'

'Asthma brand pork rinds can't miss,' a kiwi piped from below. 'Think of it! The tangy flavour of pork rinds with the everlasting goodness of Asthma . . .' He pulled something shiny out of his briefcase and thrust it towards the cat. 'I've already had the bags designed!'

But the wannabes and hangers-on were small potatoes compared to the animals who used their muscle or cunning to become Asthma's representatives. One, a gerbil, slapped the kiwi's tiny mock-ups away.

'Look, pal,' the gerbil said. 'Asthma just got here and he's tired. He doesn't want anything to do with a small-time schmuck like you, so just . . .'

Another gerbil was working the other side, moving through the crowd delivering a message. 'You wanna talk to Asthma,' he explained in a quiet but forceful voice, 'you come through me. I'll make sure he hears what you have to say – for a price.' Gerbils are known throughout the animal kingdom for their Machievellian strategising.

Asthma didn't say anything to the tumult that was going on around him. He just sat calmly, trimming his rear claws by popping them into his mouth and gnawing them.

The beavers stood at the back, hoping that they could get Asthma to kiss their Chip and Woody. Pete, Sue, and Loo, now full of cholesterol, fat, and e. coli, were arguing among themselves.

'That weeny thing can't be Asthma!' Pete said. 'Asthma's got to be impressive.'

'I don't know,' Loo said almost dreamily. 'I think I like him. Maybe he has rabies.'

Asthma certainly didn't look rabid; indeed, it was perhaps his very calmness that seemed to stoke the crowd even further. A ptarmigan made a rush for Asthma, but was intercepted by the gerbil. 'Not so fast,' the gerbil said. 'Let the man groom himself.'

Asthma was indeed licking his own fur, his head making wide, somewhat silly-looking circles. Then he stopped. For a few long seconds, Asthma just sat quietly with an odd, fixed-eyed look on his face.

'Shh,' the other gerbil said. 'I think he's about to say something!'

The whole crowd went silent, in expectation of the pearls of wisdom that surely would come. But instead of pearls, out came a huge amount of semi-digested kibble.

The crowd stayed quiet for a moment, then one animal spoke up. 'Do you not see?' a sloth said. 'Asthma wants us to spend our lives in quiet contemplation, so that we may expel what is unclean, though it may lurk deep within!'

A portion of the crowd murmured its assent.

'Folks . . .' Asthma said, but no one paid attention.

'No!' a vole cried. 'That way lies madness. Asthma is telling us to labour mightily, in ways seen and unseen, to bring forth new works, disgusting though they may be.'

'Really, I—' Asthma's voice was soon drowned out by the two factions in heated debate. In moments one gerbil had joined one and the other gerbil the other. There Asthma sat, forgotten, with the helpless, rueful look of somebody going through something unpleasant they've experienced many, many times before. Shaking his head, Asthma walked away from the crowd, which was now clearly much more intent on arguing with each other than anything he might have to say.

Asthma eventually made his way back to where the beavers and the children stood. 'What can you do?' Asthma shrugged. 'Followers.' He turned to Loo, whose hair was a geometric mass of partially-dried gravy mixed with bright-orange sweet and sour sauce. 'I see you got some food,' he said.

This reminded them all that it was time to go back for another feed. It seemed so dreadfully impolite, Sue thought, but Pete had no such misgivings. He could feel his stomach stamping his feet.

'Asthma, we're going to—' he pointed in the direction of the tent.

'Go ahead,' Asthma said, nodding. The children bolted. 'So those are the humans,' Asthma said to the beavers. 'I thought they'd be taller.'

'Are all of them like that?' Naomi asked.

'Like what?' Asthma said, bemusement in his voice.

'Like . . . that.' She pointed, and they all watched Loo plant her face at one end of a tray of baked beans and plough it forward like a piece of earth-moving equipment.

Ruth sighed. 'It's a shame we couldn't just throw them back . . .' The beavers looked at Asthma, hope in their eyes.

''Fraid not,' Asthma said. 'We might get sued for discrimination.'

'But they're illegal immigrants,' Naomi said, trailing off. She put Chip down on his end.

'Chip's so big! Already standing – how old is he?' Asthma asked.

'Erm,' Naomi fumbled. She wasn't sure whether Asthma was putting her on, humouring Ruth or just as crazy as her partner was. 'I can't remember.'

'It's been a while since we've taken them to the doctor and had their rings counted,' Ruth said. Meanwhile, the log had toppled over and began to roll away. 'Oh! Grab Chip.' She brought her face down to the log in her own arms. 'That's why Mama doesn't put you down.' Ruth made some baby talk, then rubbed noses; this ended abruptly when she got a splinter.

Under the tent, they saw an old man's head appear, sticking out of a cooler. 'Hullo, there! What's all this?'

The satyr rushed out from behind the bar, and pushed the man's head down, saying, 'Get out, you! Blarnia's invitation only!' He closed the lid, and put a jeroboam atop it.

'See, that's how we should treat wardrovers,' Naomi said.[22]

---

[22] 'Wardrover' was crude local slang for unwanted visitors to Blarnia.

'Now, that's not fair,' Asthma admonished her. 'After all, Blarnians go over to their world constantly.'

'It's not the same,' Naomi said. 'We may steal things, but we don't get involved in their politics.' (In fact, Naomi had got the idea for her dam from seeing a picture of the Hoover Dam in a stolen Earth magazine.)

'Is that how you got the tent?' Ruth asked.

'Apparently,' Asthma said. 'Somebody turned a portable cooler into a passageway to Blarnia, then stole the whole set-up from a college reunion.' The three of them looked at the beige striped tent, its sides, banner and pennants snapping in the breeze. 'I can't say as I approve of stealing from the humans' world, but since nobody here has thumbs, certain allowances—'

Naomi whipped off her necklace, installed it, then cleared her throat.

'Well, well, Naomi,' Asthma chuckled. 'I wondered how you managed to build all that stuff. With beavers like you, who needs evolution?'

Ruth cleared her throat, then said, 'Asthma, you have to come and mend that rocking chair you made for us. It's all cockeyed.'

'I'll mend it, Ruth, but it'll cost you.'

Ruth was flabbergasted. Naomi, ever the peacemaker, stepped in. 'How much will it cost?'

'Plenty,' Asthma said.

Ruth couldn't contain herself any longer. 'Oh yeah? What will you charge to never make anything for us ever again?'

Asthma rolled his eyes. 'Even more. You have no idea how grateful people are.' Seeing that Ruth was really angry, he leaned over and rubbed his head on her affectionately. 'Ruth my child, after we are finished here, go back to your home. Then all will be well.'

Ruth felt better after that. Later, they were alone for a moment, Naomi asked, 'Did you just perform a miracle?'

'No,' Asthma said, chuckling. 'I meant all will be well *for me* – 'cause I'll be gone!'

A half-hour later, after the Perversies had finished Feed Number Two, the festivities on the hilltop were definitely winding down. The children had wobbled off in different directions, to digest. The bar under the pavilion had run out of ice, and the few animals that remained there were doing shots tinged with melancholy. Perhaps that was why the earlier schism led by the gerbils had still not healed.

Asthma padded about, getting to know his followers again, trying to convince them (mostly in vain) that it didn't matter whom they preferred, the one gerbil or the other. 'Look,' he said, 'I take your point that I'm not always absolutely clear,' he said to a pair of sceptical-looking turtles, 'but I can *promise* you that I don't want you to fight about it.'

'But we like to fight,' one turtle said.

'I know, I know, that's why I'm specifically telling you not to. Look—'

'I think what Asthma's trying to say,' the other turtle said to his friend, 'is that you should never fight if you're *wrong*.'

'No! That's not what I—'

'That makes a lot of sense,' the first turtle said. 'Thanks, Asthma!'

'Yeah, thanks,' the second turtle said. They began to walk away, then he turned back for a moment. 'By the way, when are we going to fight the Wide Witch?'

Asthma didn't answer. Dispirited, he turned – just in time to see some wildebeests peeing into the Stone Bathtub. 'Don't *do* that!' Asthma yowled with irritation.

Naomi walked up. 'I saw that stuff with the turtles. The moment you get here people are already choosing sides and laying into each other. How do you stand it?'

'I have to be honest,' Asthma said, crossing his paws, 'at first it really bothered me. Then, after the billionth time it happened, I realised something: They were going to fight among themselves whether I was around

~ 185 ~

or not; perhaps what I told them would make some difference. I just hope it doesn't make things worse.'

'Of course it doesn't!' Naomi said, not stopping to think of any examples. She bent down and clapped the cat on the back. 'Cheer up: everything will be a lot easier once we have a common enemy.' Whistling, she walked away.

Asthma rolled on his back and swiped at the air in frustration.

As a male, the oldest, and someone with the creed 'eat first, and examine later,' Pete could handle more calories than Sue or Loo, and was ready for another crack at the buffet. That it was now positively post-apocalyptic in aspect, down to the dregs of the dregs, and featured items that would make a billygoat vomit, mattered not a whit to the iron-stomached proto-teen. Asthma stopped him.

'Would you like me to point out some of the sights? There's the river, and that gooey patch over there is Cair Amel . . .'

'Nah, got to eat,' Pete said, blowing Asthma off. Just as he bellied up for Feed Number Three, however, Pete heard a strange noise, a kind of ragged blatting. Figuring it was digestive in nature, Pete shrugged and began to tuck in.

Twenty feet away, Asthma was still on his back, trying to think peaceful thoughts. A goose, an octopus, and a clam walked up to him.

'Excuse me, Your . . . Furriness,' the goose said. 'We had an office pool on when you'd return to Blarnia.'

'Yeah, so?' Asthma said. The desert was nice – why had he ever left the desert?

'So, I won it,' the goose said. 'But they won't pay up. They say you should pay.'

As a cat, Asthma heard the blat even better than Pete had. 'Did any of you make that noise?'

'No,' the goose said.

Suddenly, they saw Loo skitter past. 'Somebody grab her before she impales herself,' Asthma said, reading the girl's mind.

The octopus did so.

'Squeeze harder!' Loo exhorted the octopus. 'I can still breathe.'

Then, Sue appeared, blowing on her Mardi Gras horn. Nipping at her heels and barking wildly was that breadbox full of irritating behaviour, Furious Arf.

Several animals stepped forward to dispatch the mini-canine.

'No,' Asthma said, holding up a paw. 'Let Pete do it.'

'Wha'?' Pete said. A bite of cake fell from his mouth on to his shirt. 'I'm eating.'

Asthma looked impassive.

'You can't be serious.'

Sue was now running in a circle, with the irrepress-ible irritant close behind. 'Come on, you wanker! I hate having dog-spit on me!'

Pete realised that everybody was looking at him. 'Oh, well, if you insist . . .'

'Ten quid on the dustmop,' the goose said.

'Fifty on the meathead,' the octopus said, then told the clam with a wink, 'I read ahead.'

Pete stepped into the path of the frothing Yorkie without much thought about what to do next. So the dog ended its pursuit of his sister and began chasing him.

Round and round they went. The crowd was largely dissatisfied with this strategy which, it must be ad-mitted, did not afford much of an endgame. 'Surely throwing something could only help,' Pete thought; in his opinion, nearly every situation could be improved by throwing. But what to throw?

As a prodigious stitch blossomed in his side, Pete felt his pockets. The amount of food stuck to his clothing, while substantial, did not seem to be enough to com-pose a distracting treat. He felt in his pockets – and discovered the pink squeaky bone that Father Xmas had given to him. Suddenly, he knew what he must do.

'Here, boy!' Pete called, taking the bone out and waggling it. He squeezed it a couple of times and Furious was fascinated. Running to the edge of the hilltop, Pete gave the toy a mighty heave in the direction of the river. 'Go – *get it*!'

Not waiting to hear the splash, the miniature Yorkshire terrier sped off in the direction of the throw. Pete saw the toy hit the silver river far below, then bob to the surface. The dog raced to the edge of the river, frothy and brackish from all the melting snow, and leapt in without a second thought. He had courage, one had to give him that.

By now, the crowd had gathered around Pete, and everyone was peering down at the river below. They saw Furious swimming for all he was worth, intent on the rubber toy dancing on the currents just ahead. 'Go, Furious! Go Furious! Go Furious!' they chanted. When he reached it, a great, ragged cheer went up – and then a groan, as the exhausted Furious slipped beneath the waves with a faint, almost plaintive 'blorp.'

At that moment, another toy dog appeared at the crown of the hill, attracted by the cheering, and wondering if there was some food in it for him somehow.

'There's another of her guard dogs!' the other gerbil yelled. 'Let's cook it! After him!'

The dog turned and scampered for its life. Several of Asthma's more hot-headed followers took off after it

Ordeal over, Asthma walked over to Pete. 'Pete, kneel.'

Tired, Pete was only too happy to comply, but Asthma was still too short. 'Okay, I think you'll have to lie on the ground.'

Pete did so. Asthma borrowed a barbecued drumstick from a nymph standing nearby.

'Hey!' the nymph said.

'I'll give it back,' Asthma said. The cat touched Pete with the drumstick, smearing his shoulder with barbecue sauce. 'Rise, Sir Pete Furious-Bone—'

'That should help him get dates,' Naomi mumbled to Ruth with a smirk.

'—rise, and get me a few more drumsticks. These things smell surprisingly good.'

CHAPTER 13

 And what was Ed doing during all of this, you ask? (Even if you didn't, let us pretend you did.) Feeling sorry for himself, mostly, and swearing that, if he got out of this alive, he'd make an anti-drug commercial.

'Hi, kids. My name is Ed Perversie,' Ed rehearsed in his head. 'Earlier this year I went into a wardrobe, and mistakenly ingested some banana-peel extract. I went to a strange new land, full of exotic creatures and dangerous adventures. Sounds fun, right?

'Wrong. What I found in Blarnia were a bunch of morons, each more disgusting than the last. And those were just my siblings! But seriously, folks . . .'

The Wide Witch boxed Ed's ear. 'Shut up, and be more miserable!' she barked.

'As I was saying,' the dwarf said, 'I have a cousin who's a djinn and also an accountant. Maybe he can . . .'

'Enough!' the Wide Witch said haughtily. 'Financial matters bore me. Let's stop here, and further the plot.' The trio halted in a small valley. Like all valleys after the great melting, it was filled with detritus, by which I mean the bloated carcasses of woodland creatures surprised mid-procreate by the torrential run-off.

'At least they died doing what they loved,' the dwarf said.

Ed was hungry, thirsty, sweaty, smelly, footsore, mud-streaked, tone-deaf, itchy and petulant. Luckily for the Wide Witch, he was also too tired to complain about any of these things. He drop-kicked a stiffening vole and flopped down on the ground.

'I'm famished,' the Wide Witch said, checking her perspiration-dark clothes for a food of some kind. 'I want a treat,' she said. 'I need a treat – I can feel myself getting smaller!'

'P.U.,' the dwarf said to Ed, plugging his nostrils with his long beard. 'Son of Atom, you actually make dead animals smell good. You need a bath!'

The Witch's eyes lit up with an idea. 'Dwarf, tie this entrée to a tree.'

'Your Majesty, there's still no rope.'

'Damn it, man, use your imagination!' she hollered.

Feeling rather stupid, the dwarf hauled Ed to his feet and mimed lashing him to a tree with an imaginary rope. Ed was too tired to put up a fight.

'Okay, now, stand back,' the Witch said. She aimed her wand at Ed and a jet of cold water came out of it.

'Oh, yeah,' Ed said. He was hot and sweaty and muck-covered after the hike, so the water was quite refreshing.

As soon as she realised he was enjoying it, the Wide Witch shut the water off immediately by twisting a little knob at the end of her wand. Ed immediately dropped back into the twilight of his exhaustion. The Wide Witch twisted the knob again, and two sharp prongs came out of the end. She took a step towards Ed with malice aforethought.

'I wonder,' the dwarf said, 'might you save me some of the sweetbreads?'

Just as the Wide Witch was about to backhand the dwarf for his insolence, an exhausted toy Yorkie bounded into the clearing.

'Yap! Your Majesty!' the dog said. 'He is here!'

'I think it's pretty affected to talk about yourself in the third person,' the dwarf said, aiming a kick.

'Who?' the Wide Witch said.

'Him! The (yip! yap!) cat! Asthma!' The dog began sniffing Ed's shoes, preparing to pee. Ed was so weak that he didn't even shoo the dog away.

'Oh, right,' the Wide Witch said. 'Sorry. Low blood sugar.'

'(yip) The Son of Atom killed Furious Arf, by —'

The Wide Witch waved her hand. 'I don't need to

know the details. I'm sure it was something very stupid,' she said. 'Go and gather all our forces, so that we might mount a pointless frontal attack against vastly superior forces led by the hero of the book.'

The dog scampered off.

'That's an awfully good plan,' the dwarf simpered sarcastically. 'I don't see how it could possibly fail.'

As usual, it went over the Witch's head. 'It's in my contract,' the Wide Witch said with a shrug. The distractions gone, she turned back towards Ed, who was still tied to the tree. Shake, shake, shake went the salt shaker over Ed's head. The tapping of the tiny crystals on his noggin were his death knell. Ask not for whom the shaker shakes . . . As the dwarf tied the blindfold around his eyes, Ed wondered for a moment if something kinky was about to happen. Then, in a flash, he realised just what was in store for him, and desperately played for time.

'Sorry my brother killed your dog,' Ed said. 'He's always killing pets. He says it's a mistake, but it's totally not. One time, my sister had this budgerigar, and Pete was was giving himself a hickey with Mum's vacuum cleaner, and . . .'

'Silence!' the Wide Witch said. 'Your gross reminiscing is affecting my appetite.'

'Wait, wait, I have a joke to tell you – it's really

funny, you can't kill me before you hear the punch-line . . .' The Witch paid no attention. She ground some pepper over Ed, then smeared a great glob of HP Sauce on his hair. Ed thought of all the good people in his life, and even though that was a depressingly short list, he still shed a tear. Then the Wide Witch raised her fork . . . and all hell (or was it heaven?) broke loose.

First, Ed heard the Wide Witch question someone's parentage, and the dwarf squeal in terror. Then shouts, sporadic gunfire, loud rock music and (he wasn't sure) a small marching band.

'Stay still,' a rough but kind voice said. Then a rough but kind claw snipped the imaginary rope tying him to the tree. 'Eww, you're all wet,' someone said roughly but kindly.

Ed sunk to his knees, then ripped off his blindfold and looked around. An immense fiddler crab had been the agent of Ed's salvation, so Ed felt ever so slightly bad about wondering whether fiddler crab tasted like lobster, and further, whether anybody would miss the crab.

'Give him a shot,' a big black bear said.

A cow wearing spectacles handed him one of Ms Beaver's custom-carved sombrero-shaped shotglasses. 'Here you go.'

The booze was homemade, and burned like the devil going down. Ed didn't know whether to say thanks or not – luckily, his choking made the question moot. The cow smacked him on the back with her hoof.

A menagerie milled about, looking for the Wide Witch and her driver. There they stood, right in the middle of everything, totally unobserved.

'They must have got away,' the bear said dejectedly. Blarnia was a land as yet unsullied by optometry, and so most creatures suffered through life with very poor vision. Even sharp-eyed creatures like eagles learned to hide their skill after eons of peer-pressure.

'It certainly looks like it,' the cow said, shaking her head sadly. As a glasses-wearer, she was considered to be a dangerous free-thinker. But since they had been carved by Ms Beaver, the lenses were made of solid wood. The cow scanned the scene, then squinted over her glasses, just to be sure. 'That Witch certainly has powerful magic.'

'What?' Ed cried. 'Don't you see them? They're right there!' Ed jabbed his finger frenziedly. The Witch and the dwarf tried to wave him off, silently mouthing the word 'No.' Ed paid no attention. 'They're in front of you!' he said. They could end this book right now, if only . . .

'Anybody see anything?' the bear called to the rest,

who were idly punching trees and wrestling tufts of wet grass to the ground in shows of frustrated aggression.

'No-oo,' the crowd chorused, including a possum who actually bumped into the Wide Witch.

'Hey, watch it,' the Wide Witch said.

'Sorry,' the possum said meekly.

An extended monologue on the topic of frustration died in Ed's throat; he simply didn't have enough energy. 'Look there,' Ed said wearily. 'Those two shapes. Next to all the footprints.' He had no expectation of success.

The bear squinted. 'Looks like a tree and a – rubbish bin or something. Are you a tree?' he asked the Wide Witch.

'No,' she said. 'I'm a piece of modern art.'

'Oh,' the bear said. 'Never understood modern art.' He turned to Ed. 'See? It's just a piece of modern art and a' – the dwarf sneezed – 'sneezing rubbish bin.'

'God bless you,' the cow said.

'Screw you,' the dwarf said, wiping his nose.

And with that, the bear scooped Ed up and plopped him onto the cow's broad, slightly furry back. 'To the Stone Bathtub!' he roared. A great cheer went up, and the cow headed off at a brisk trot.

'Watch out for that—' Ed ducked under a low-hanging tree branch.

The cow didn't. She was knocked cold, and Ed had to walk all the way back.

Presently the rescue party ambled back to the hill where Asthma and the others were encamped. The Perversie children had slept under the buffet table, growling whenever anybody came near it. When Ed arrived, they let him through – he knew all their tricks, and could fight just as dirtily as they could.

It was not a friendly homecoming – not that Ed cared, as long as they left him alone long enough to fill his belly.

'That was deuced treacherous of you,' Pete said, as he and his brother circled each other. 'Selling out to the other squad like that . . . Hey, was that the last potato croquette?'

''Fraid so,' Ed said. Not that he'd been afraid of Pete before, but his sojourn with the Wide Witch had made him more confident somehow. 'Look, think what you want, but I thought she had food.'

Sue, who was wrestling with Loo over a plastic fork, piped up, 'That's no reason to—'

Suddenly, the small and not at all majestic form of Asthma appeared at the entrance to the pavilion. 'Loo, stop trying to kill yourself,' he commanded. 'Ed, we need to talk.'

'One second.' Ed grabbed a now-stale baguette and stuffed it into one pocket, then scooped up some butter pats and dropped them into the other.

'No rush,' Asthma said. As the two of them left, Pete got annoyed at how nicely Asthma was treating Ed.

'Be sure to punish him, Asthma!' Pete yelled after the pair. 'Don't forget!' Then Pete said to his sisters, 'I hope Ed has to suffer for his mistakes. That would be corking fun to watch.'

Asthma paid no attention to Pete's demands; his relationship with Ed was none of Pete's business. Now, as I am sure you are aware, some authors have the irritating habit of discreetly drawing a curtain over events that they deem too sensitive or embarrassing to relate. But it is eminently clear that there is no point in writing books without the embarrassing parts in them, because that is exactly what people want to read about. Literature is gossip about imaginary people, and it is not fair to leave out the juicy bits, simply because of 'decorum' or 'morals' or 'basic human decency.' So we will join Ed's conversation with Asthma, already in progress.

'. . . so what *is* the meaning of life?'

'Oh, I can't tell you that,' Asthma said teasingly. 'You'd laugh.' Asthma changed the subject. 'How's school? Where do you go, again?'

Ed told Asthma.

'Really? I thought that one was condemned, after the national test scores came back. Or was it the one they turned into a prison, to cut out the middleman?' Asthma asked. 'Anyway, about the Witch: You know she's a jerk, right?'

'I found that out eventually,' Ed admitted. He buttered a bit of bread and ate it.

'Give me one of those pats,' Asthma said. Ed took the foil from one and placed it on the ground. Asthma licked it as they talked.

'Thank you,' Asthma said. 'Well, live and learn. You're not the first guy who thought with his—'

'Wallet, I know. Oh, you mean my . . . ? It wasn't just that,' Ed said, blushing. 'When I met her, she seemed so . . . upwardly mobile. And she treated me so much better than my stupid brother and sisters. I'm sick of them picking on me, just because they have no ambition or intelligence . You don't know what it's like,' Ed complained. 'All the people you're related to are saints and stuff.'

'I don't know about sibling rivalry?' Asthma asked. 'What do you think my siblings did when Mum told them who my Dad was? First, they told everybody I was adopted, then they told everybody I was stuck up . . . Of course, I can't blame them. I had a later bedtime, I didn't have to do chores . . . They used to torment me. Until I made their _____ fall off.' He laughed at the memory.

'I wish I could do that to my brother and sisters,' Ed said. 'Think of the good it would do humanity. Come on – I bet you can do it just by pointing.' Ed fished a crumpled five pound note out of his pocket. 'It's yours – just try.'

'No,' Asthma said, laughing again. It was only later that Ed realised how strange it was to hear a cat laugh. 'Ed,' Asthma said, 'being clever is a good thing, but it's not the only thing. Everybody has their talents. Everybody has something to offer.'

'Even my brother and sisters?'

'Except for them. No, just kidding.'

'Name one thing.'

Asthma paused, then added rather hastily, 'I'm sure something will come to me later, but that's not the point. The Editor-Behind-the-Scenes gives everyone the right to live unmolested, and it's not their job to prove anything to you. If you pay close enough attention, you'll discover they're not that bad. And if they are that bad, go ahead and make rude comments – just keep out of earshot.'

'Easy for you to say,' Ed grumbled. 'Everything's easy for you.'

'I take it you've never seen my carpentry.' Just then, another 'rescue party' straggled back rowdy and triumphant, loaded down with things they had 'rescued' from the supporters of the Wide Witch. The leader of the party, a rather portly roan horse, ran up to Asthma, as bubbly and jubilant as a little foal.

'Look, Asthma,' the horse said. 'Look at all the things we've liberated in your name.'

'Oh, for my sake,' Asthma said. 'What do you have all over you?'

'Fhoul's entrails,' the horse said, a bit quieter. 'We came upon them, in their sleep.'

'And you killed them?' Asthma asked sternly.

'Well, yes. We couldn't liberate their stuff without – after all, they're only fhouls—'

'Which you killed.'

'Now, see, I thought you might feel that way,' the horse said, stammering a bit. 'The way I figure it, I was just being kind. If the Afterlife is so great – which we all agree it is – I thought the kindest thing I could ever do was to send them there early.'

'You're missing my point,' Asthma said.

'Eternal life, no more suffering, no more worry, no more sore backs or headaches or dandruff,' the horse said. 'Obviously I did them a tremendous favour. And even if they had lived, things were about to get very hard for them, now that we're back in control. Even you must see that. We've been oppressed for a hundred years. It's our turn to—'

Asthma gave an angry yowl. 'Enough! We'll talk about this later.'

The horse continued talking. 'I mean, people call it "ethnic cleansing," but it's simply things returning to how they—'

'I SAID "ENOUGH"!'

The horse turned and cantered away sullenly. 'No wonder you always die,' he muttered.

'I heard that!' Asthma yelled.

When they returned to the pavilion, the Witch's dwarf was chatting amiably with the Perversie children. 'It's just a job, you know?' he said. He took a crumpled piece of paper out of his jerkin, and handed it to Sue. 'You look like the . . . least irresponsible. Could you give my CV to Asthma?'

'Give it to him yourself,' Sue said, pointing.

The dwarf turned and saw Pete. 'Here—'

Pete didn't say anything, he just pointed downward at the cat, which cleared its throat.

'Oh! Sorry!' the dwarf stammered, embarrassed. 'I never know what shape you're going to take.'

'Well, nobody quite got it the last time, so I decided

to be something unimpressive and unfairly maligned,'
Asthma said. 'Totally "meek it up," you know?'

'Very wise, very wise,' the dwarf said, then turned to
the Perversie children. 'You are very lucky to have
such a wise and noble leader.'

'Enough flattery. What is your message, Son of
Girth?'

The dwarf blushed, then said, 'Your Felineness, my
current employer the Wide Witch – I'm a long-term
temp, actually . . . I was just talking to this Daughter
of Steve about whether there might be any job
opportunities . . .'

'Talk to the gerbils,' Asthma said. 'Anything else?'

'My employer – my *current* employer—'

'You already said that,' Pete said with irritation.

'She wants to talk with you.' He grabbed a used
napkin and waved it like a white flag. 'Parley, safe
passage, all that.'

'I understand,' Asthma said. 'Tell her I agree, as long
as she takes the batteries out of her wand, and puts
them on the ground, where I can see them.'

'What if she has extras?' Sue whispered.

'It's all right,' Ed said. 'I read ahead.'

'Am I the only one who's *not* reading ahead?' Asthma
cried. 'Go!'

The dwarf scuttled away, and presently, the Wide

Witch hove into view, looking all the world like an iceberg, only less useful.

Slowly, sweating profusely in the new heat, the Wide Witch approached Asthma. Any reasonably edible animals scattered, desperate to be out-of-range of her cruel and expert fork. She stood in front of Asthma, dwarfing the small cat like a minivan parked in front of a pack of playing cards.

'You have a traitor there,' the Wide Witch said, pointing at Ed.

Ed made a rude gesture.

'"Traitor"?' Asthma asked. 'He's a citizen of the United Kingdom, dearie, not Blarnia. And anyway: if you're the Queen of Blarnia, how can helping you make him a traitor?'

'Oooo! Burn!' the crowd murmured.

Asthma shushed them. 'Of course, if you're saying you're *not* the Queen . . .'

The Wide Witch got a harassed look on her face. 'Now I remember what it's like talking to you. It always gives me a freaking headache.' She mopped her brow. 'Loser, then – will you accept that he's a loser?'

'Must admit she's got you there,' Pete said, elbowing his brother, who spat on his shoe.

Sue, in a shocking (for her) display of unruliness, chucked a butter-pat at the massive royal. It bounced off the side of the Witch's head. The dwarf, knowing she could no more bend down to grab it than she could do fifty bunny hops, scrambled over, picked it up, and handed it to her.

'Thank you,' she said, unwrapping it and popping it into her mouth.

'They're all pretty unpleasant, actually,' Asthma said. 'Seems unfair to single Ed out.'

'Hey!' the other Perversies shouted. Loo, blinded by anger and sensing the Witch's lethal power, made a dash at her. Sue grabbed Loo's collar and held her struggling, Thanatos-infused sibling back.

The Witch saw the eight-year-old's struggles and hissed, 'Bring it on.' Then to Asthma she said, 'You clearly cannot control the mob that has gathered in your name. Let us talk privately.'

'People, go and amuse yourselves for a while,' Asthma said to the crowd. 'Work on the cheers I taught you. If you do a pyramid, remember: smaller animals on top . . . And please, no more schisms.'

The crowd moved, slowly and definitely unwillingly, as there really wasn't much to do in Blarnia and this conversation would, it seemed, prove mildly entertaining. But Asthma was used to grumbling.

After they were alone, the conversation resumed. 'The best way to identify the real sleazebags in any society is to let them do it for you,' Asthma said. 'People who go around shouting "traitor" – sleazebags, every last one of them.'

'Always with the wisdom,' the Witch spat. 'Don't you ever get tired of yourself? Anyway, we both know, the boy is mine. Or perhaps you have forgotten the Cheap Magic?'

Asthma's ears swivelled back – the hippos had toppled the pyramid again – then forward again. 'If you're referring to spurious literary devices,' he said, 'designed to add cheap drama to a story, I am well aware of that.'

'They are not spurious!' The Witch howled with rage. 'Life has certain rules, and . . . where would we be if everybody ignored senseless, arbitrary agreements that they had nothing to do with?'

'In heaven, I'd expect,' Asthma said.

'We can't just live sensible, quiet lives to our own liking!' the Witch declared. 'We have to have a set of rules that everyone must follow, whether they like them or not.'

'It's not the rule itself that is important, but the reasons for the rule,' Asthma said. 'If the reasons for the rule are good, then the rule itself must be judged. Is it just? Not just proportionate, but kind? Intelligent? Wise? Each of us must weigh this for ourselves – there is no hiding behind custom or the crowd. Unjust rules must be broken, so they can be mended into a better form.'

'And that's why you always fail,' the Witch said acidly. 'No matter how many times you come back, you never play by the rules. You think you're special—'

'I think everybody's special.'

'—but you're not. Look at you! Even when you don't have any clothes, you still look like crap! You're all dusty. You're always broke. You always end up a bum, and everybody can't wait to get rid of you.'

Asthma shrugged.

'As far as the Cheap Magic is concerned, you can take it up with the Editor-Behind-the-Scenes, not me,' the Witch said. 'I want my boy tenderloin.' The Witch suddenly got a devilish grin. 'Of course the boy could be spared, if . . .'

'How?' Asthma asked. Ed was the only even mildly interesting person he'd met since arriving in Blarnia.

'If you'd give me the boy's weight in pudding,' she said. 'I'll get into the Stone Bathtub, and you can pour it all over me.' She was ecstatic. 'I'll eat my way to freedom!'

Asthma frowned, which was accentuated by the tabby markings on his forehead. 'I don't think the Editor-Behind-the-Scenes would allow that.'

'Now who's hiding behind rules?' the Witch said bitterly.

'I have another proposition,' Asthma said.

Presently Asthma returned to the pavilion, where his followers were engaged in a bitter sectarian dispute over whether pom-pons and bullhorns had to be distributed strictly along gender lines.

'What took you so long?' Ed said.

'Nothing.' Asthma never took a straight line anywhere. In this case, he'd been distracted by the shadow of a butterfly, which he chased for a while.

'So I'll have to go with her, won't I?' Ed said. It was amazing how something that had once been his most fervent hope now seemed like a terribly unappetising prospect. 'I can't believe I used to like her.'

'You're in luck,' Asthma said. 'You won't have to go.'

'What happened? How did you convince her?'

'Don't worry about it,' Asthma said, and ran off to chew a dandelion.

'Okay,' Ed said, only too happy to do so. He went back to collecting pebbles to throw at his siblings. Oh, there's a good pointy one, he said to himself.

CHAPTER 14

 As soon as the Witch had cleared off (it took a while, because she was huffing and puffing and wheezing and occasionally clutching trees for support), Asthma called everybody into the pavilion and said, 'We're moving camp.'

'Do we have to?' a dormouse said. 'It stinks everywhere else.'

'Yes, we have to,' Asthma said. 'We're going to the Fords of Bazooka.'

Grumbling only slightly more than usual, the animals and mythological creatures put their factional struggling aside for the moment and packed up the camp. Soon, they were all on their way, walking to the Fords. Presently Loo scampered over to Asthma.

'Asthma! Asthma! Asthma! Asthma! Asthma!' she called.

'Yes, Loo?' Asthma said, trying to be patient.

'Ed says you're a thinly veiled allegory. Are you?'

'Maybe,' Asthma said, blushing under his fur. 'Can you tell who I'm supposed to be?'

Loo nodded slowly, indicating 'no idea.'

'Let me give you a hint,' Asthma said. 'When I was a person, I had many followers . . . People still remember me, even though I died a long time ago . . . Should I keep going?'

Loo nodded yes, completely at a loss.

'They still talk about me. Many books have been written about what I said and did.'

'Hmm . . .' Loo said, thinking hard but coming up empty. 'What did you look like?'

'I had long hair.'

Loo stared at Asthma blankly. Asthma, a being of infinite patience, realised that there wasn't enough time in the universe to play this game. He went on: 'Listen, okay: two words, first word five letters long . . .' He paused, waiting for Loo to get it.

Nothing.

Finally, Asthma blurted out, 'It begins with "J" and ends with "S"!'

With that, comprehension broke out beatifically all over Loo's face. 'JANIS!' she yelled. 'You were Janis Joplin? Wow! Can I have your autograph?'

'Maybe later.'

Pete showed up. 'Get lost, Loo,' he said.

'Okay!' Loo said, and skittered off.

'I didn't mean that literally,' he called after his sister. 'Hey, Asthma.'

'Hey, Pete.'

'So . . .' Pete said, trying to act casual. 'When are we going to *crush* 'em?'

'Uh . . . that's not really the plan, Pete,' Asthma said. 'Not my style.'

'Right, right,' Pete said. 'Everybody says you're really boring and stuck up, that you've got no sense of humour, but I say to them, "No, it's just really . . ."'

'Dry?'

'Yeah, dry. Like when it's funny but not really. Deadpan,' Pete said. 'So when are we going to march on the Witch's castle?' Pete was bouncing up and down a little as he walked; the boy took a tiny straw he'd swiped from the bar inside the pavilion, and mimed a dramatic swordfight with an invisible enemy. Pete could make a weapon out of anything. 'Ooh, can I be in the front? You saw how I did with Furious Arf – I promise to kill a *lot* of 'em—'

'You'll do nothing of the sort!' Asthma said firmly, fur bristling. 'There'll be no attacking and no killing as long as I'm in charge!'

Pete stopped swordfighting, genuinely puzzled. 'But – then how – the gerbils said that—'

'I don't care what the gerbils said.' Asthma's tail swished back and forth in irritation. 'Go and follow the gerbils if you want. Or somebody else, I don't care.

The Chronicles of Blarnia

But if you want to . . .' (At this point Asthma paused, looking for a metaphor that Pete would really understand.) '. . . be on my team, you had better follow my rules. And Rule Number One is: No killing.'

Pete made a crestfallen noise.

'You know what Rule Number Two is? Also, "No killing." And Rule Number Three – you guessed it –'

'It's Opposites Day!' Pete offered hopefully.

'NO KILLING! And if you have any energy left over after that, love your enemy. And, whenever possible, help the poor and the despised. There's plenty of others, but that'll do for now. Go and work on those, and when you've got them down cold, come see me and I'll give you some more. Got it?'

Pete looked for all the world like he'd just been informed that professional wrestling was fake. Then a smile creased the lower half of his stolid features. 'I get it . . .' he said.

'Good!' Asthma said with relief. 'Now go and tell all the others, explaining it over and over drives me crazy.'

'. . . you're planning a sneak attack! Is it going to be just you, commando-style, or can I come? I can be very quiet, and I'll draw on my face in marker to hide better, and – Loo tells me you have superpowers. Do you have heat-vision? Can I see it? Are you planning to use that in the sneak attack?'

Rather than hiss at the lad, Asthma excused himself, dropping back to be with the two Perversie girls. He stayed with Sue and Loo for the rest of the journey. They thought he seemed rather sad.

'Is everything all right?' Sue asked the cat. 'Aren't you happy to be back in Blarnia?'

'Of course I am,' Asthma said. 'It's just that whenever I think somebody's finally understood, it turns out they haven't at all.'

'Do you threaten them?' Sue asked. 'The teachers at my school do it all the time. I don't think I'd ever learn *anything* if they didn't threaten to strike or humiliate me.'

Presently, the party arrived at a place where the river was broad and shallow, and the mud surrounding it was bright pink and exceedingly sticky.

'All right, everybody, stop! These are the Fords of Bazooka!'

A cassowary stood, attempting to free his claws from the pink muck. 'You're kidding – we're stopping here?'

'Yes, indeed. No enemy could catch us by surprise here on the Fords of Bazooka,' Asthma said. And this was true, even if it was equally true that they themselves would be ensnared.

'It's like he doesn't want to fight,' Pete grumbled,

picking some pink mud out of his hair. 'Or maybe that's what he wants the enemy to think!'

'Loo, don't put that in your mouth!' Sue said, slapping the handful already en route.

'But everyone's doing it,' she whined. And it was true – all the animals had begun to chew the mud and blow big pink bubbles with it. Some had even found strange bushes that in place of leaves sprouted little comics. The jokes weren't very funny, but it was still miraculous.

'And I suppose if everybody jumped off a bridge . . .' Sue realised the stupidity of that rhetorical question and – for once – gave up. Loo chewed along with everybody else. The evening was spent in quiet conversation, and after Loo had received her fourteenth Heimlich the Perversie children decided to turn in.

Pete and Ed, being unnecessary to the plot, dropped off immediately. Their sisters, however, found sleep elusive. It is often the case that rest is hardest to come by when its necessity is the greatest; the girls' minds were turned towards the surely momentous day ahead.

'I feel that something dreadful is about to happen,' Sue said.

'Serves you right for reading ahead,' Loo replied, truly beating the joke to death. Then she brightened. 'Do you think it might be dangerous?'

'I don't know,' Sue said worriedly. 'I think so.'

Loo clapped her hands. 'Goody!' That was it for sleep that night. As one girl wrestled with vague forebodings, the other spun ever-more-feverish fantasies of self-extinguishing. After it was clear neither girl was going to sleep, Loo suggested they take a walk. Sue didn't want to – she thought she heard someone speaking in a Srebnian accent – but after Loo had bolted outside, all Sue could do was follow.

The moonlight was bright, but that didn't stop Loo from ploughing right into a thicket of poison ivy. She began rolling around in it, then stuffing it into her mouth with both hands.

'Loo, you can't die from that,' Sue said, pulling Loo's hand away from her mouth. 'Look!' The girls froze – there, in the pale light, they saw Asthma emerge from the tiny pavilion that covered his litter box.

Asthma stopped, sniffed the air, then walked into the forest at a slow pace.

'I wonder where he's going?' Loo asked. 'Let's follow him.'

'Let's not and say we did,' Sue said. But the involuntary spasm that followed all Loo's bad ideas had already kicked in, so her sister had already started after the small cat. 'Okay, but let's be quiet,' Sue said. 'We don't want him to send us back to bed.'

In the darkness of the wood, Asthma was quite difficult to see. Sue and Loo had to train their eyes to follow the small spray of white fur on Asthma's chest. One hardly noticed it in the daytime, but in the night, it shone like a tiny bit of faerie fire.

Up ahead, the cat wound through the underbrush slowly, almost resentfully. 'Always dying,' he said. 'There has to be a better way to make a living.' Asthma stopped, turning an ear in the direction of the girls. They stopped, too. There was a long second, then Asthma called to them.

'Hello, children,' he said. 'Why are you following me?'

'How did you know we were following you?' Loo asked.

'Well, first there was the crashing around in the poison ivy, then there was Loo twisting her ankle in the mole's hole, then Sue's tripping over the rotting log and falling down into the small gorge and screaming at the dead animal she almost landed on mouth-first, then . . .' Asthma didn't mention the whiffiness generated by two young humans who hadn't bathed since before the beginning of the book. He was indeed kind.

'All right, we get the point,' Sue said. 'Where are you going?'

'I can't tell you. Anyway, it's likely to be—' Asthma

was going to say 'dangerous,' but then realised who he was talking to '—rather silly.'

'Is anyone likely to get hurt?' Loo asked.

'No,' Asthma lied.

'What if they really, really tried?' Loo pushed.

'Probably not even then,' Asthma said. He gave a large stage-wink in Sue's direction, to let her know that she'd have to be on suicide-watch again.

Sue got the hint – but then, she'd have to do that back at the camp, too. They might as well do something interesting in the meantime. 'May we come with you?' Sue asked.

Asthma shrugged. 'It's a free country, now that I'm here. But you must promise that you'll turn back when I tell you to.'

'Oh we will,' the girls said. 'We promise.'

Asthma knew they were lying; he could see inside the hearts of all creatures – perhaps that's why he was frequently depressed. Oh well, he thought, it'll be no worse than a violent video game, and maybe they'll learn something. 'Then we must proceed quickly,' Asthma said. 'Much has to happen before morning comes again.'

Though it was dark, Asthma picked his way through the still-drippy tangles of the forest with ease. The humans, being much bigger (and clumsy besides), kept up as best they could. Every so often, Asthma would pause, tail wrapped around his feet, so that they could catch up. The group made small talk as they walked in the moonlight.

'So if you could take any shape you chose, why did you come to Blarnia as a weeny little moggie?' Sue said.

'And why not a nicer colour, like ginger or tortoise-shell?' Loo asked.

'No offence,' Sue added nervously.

Asthma laughed. 'I don't take it personally,' he said. 'What's outside is not so important. Look at Loo—' The girl was already breaking out from the poison ivy, and the weeping sores glistened in the moonlight. 'No matter how crusty and disgusting her outside gets, she's still the same inside, where it counts.' Asthma paused, and let them crash through the underbrush to catch up. 'I thought about coming to Blarnia as something strong and powerful, like an armoured sperm whale for example. Wouldn't that have been cool? Then I realized that might give people the wrong message. Creatures here are extremely simple – you can't expect them to understand anything at all. If I came back as, say, a huge, fearsome lion, they might think that the most important thing was to be grand, and proud, and fierce, when that's not the point at all.'

Sue piped up. 'Is it true that the grander a person is

here, the harder it is to please the Editor-Behind-the-Scenes later?'

'We're all weeny little rotters compared to him,' Asthma said. 'If I had come back as a lion, people might even think that I wanted them to be like lions, consuming the weak and the old, ruling by violence, by tooth and claw.'

Sue snorted. 'Do you really think people would be stupid enough to think that?'

'You'd be amazed at what people can convince themselves of,' the cat said, 'when it suits their vanity. So I decided to come back as something small and soft, something you'd never think was powerful. Ignorant people even kill black cats, because they think they're evil. Despised but unbowed – that's my type of animal.'

'I think you should've come back as a big shark, with a jar of seawater on its head so it could breathe. And bombs, that you could throw!' Loo said loudly.

'Loo, small things can be powerful, too,' Sue said, ever the older sister. 'Remember the time you swallowed that hornet?'

Now that her eyes had adjusted fully to the lack of light, Sue began to recognise their surroundings. They were headed back to the hill, and the Stone Bathtub. When they reached the lip of it, Asthma turned and said, 'This is my stop. Why don't you go back to the camp now?'

'What if we don't want to?' Loo said brattily.

'I'd really prefer it if you did,' Asthma said. 'What's about to take place will almost surely be . . . embarrassing.'

'Of course we'll turn back,' Sue lied.

'Then farewell,' Asthma said. He gave each girl a small, rough lick. The cat walked a few steps, then turned around. 'You're still here,' he said.

'I know,' Sue said, scrambling for an excuse. 'I just . . . had a stone in my shoe.'

'Okay,' Asthma said, not turning around this time.

The girls saw the game that was being played, and began walking backwards, towards the forest. 'Okay, Asthma, bye!' they said fakely. 'Bye!' As soon as they were convinced the cat was out of earshot, they crept back to the lip of the hill, and secreted themselves behind a small hedge there. Asthma knew exactly what they had done, but couldn't bother himself with that now. He had a climactic scene to do.

The Wide Witch and her minions were sitting around playing gin rummy. The game was lit by several Tiki-headed torches driven into the ground and they threw creepy shadows over the nightspawn that had apparently gathered, to chat, unwind, and see Asthma get done over. A bit further away, a few mini-giants were huddled around a charcoal grill, flipping incredibly evil hamburgers.

'Well, well,' the Wide Witch crowed when Asthma came into view. 'We didn't think you were going to show up. We were just about to play Ultimate Frisbee.' The infernal colleagues that surrounded her cackled sinisterly. A love of Ultimate Frisbee was just part of their thoroughly diabolical nature.

There were ogres and voguers, minotaurs and senataurs, effetes, sporknies and crettins. There were soupy gruels and sloppy sags, the spirits of evil trees and the spirits of even eviller grass clippings collected into bags for easier transport. Incubi and succubi read dirty incunabulae to howling denizens of dark places who never, ever brushed their teeth. And there were some creatures too awful for me to describe without receiving additional payment.

Head held high and whiskers twitching, Asthma padded into the middle of them, utterly unafraid. 'Let's get this over with,' he said.

'Bind him,' the Wide Witch said. Four sags approached, breasts trailing along the ground, and tied Asthma up. 'There is no need to restrain me,' Asthma said. 'I'm doing this freely.' But not even Asthma could resist batting and leaping at the dangling cords.

'Stop! This isn't supposed to be fun for *you*,' the Witch spat. Then she clapped her hands and said, 'Give him his summer haircut!'

Several crettins approached, brandishing clippers. As they set to work shearing off Asthma's fine black coat, the Wide Witch said, 'Now you've made it warm, I expect you'll want to be cooler.' She directed the crettins: 'Be sure to leave his ruff – and a pompon on every foot.'

'May I leave a ball at the end of his tail?' one asked.

The Witch laughed aloud. 'Oh, definitely.'

Asthma gave a small meow, then hid it by clearing his throat.

'Stop feeling sorry for yourself,' she said, pulling down her ludicrously small 'Blarnia is for Lovers' t-shirt. 'If we all must look like idiots because of the heat, you're surely going to join us.'

Back at the edge of the hill, the girls stared in horror. 'Oh, I can't look,' Sue said, watching intently. 'He looks so miserable.' Sue and Loo watched the shaving from between spread fingers.

Finally, it was done. Then the Witch cried, 'Fill the tub!'

The effetes lisped out a spell, and the Stone Bathtub was filled with hot, soapy water. They clapped their hands, and a smelly old sag picked Asthma up and carried him to the tub. Triumphant, the Wide Witch bellowed, 'Bathe the cat!'

Sue and Loo watched in amazement as Asthma allowed himself to be plopped into the bath, with nary a yowl. They kept expecting him to scratch and bite his assailants, to leap out of the tub and make a dash for freedom, but he did not. Asthma simply sat quietly – though certainly unhappily – as the now jubilant crowd of baddies filed past, each giving him a scrub.

After he had been shampooed and conditioned, Asthma was brought out of the Stone Bathtub. The girls saw that he looked even smaller than usual, scrawny even. They dried him off with the Stone Towel, then finished the job using the Stone Blowdryer.

'And now for the coup de grace,' the Wide Witch said in a low and menacing voice. She clapped her hands. 'Bring me the dolly clothes!'

The girls watched as a flower-print shift was pulled over Asthma's head, and an absurd pink bonnet roughly slapped on him, smushing his ears. The cat looked miserable, as all animals do when the grace and beauty of their natural form is altered.

But worse, much worse, was to come. For now a checked picnic cloth was spread over the ground. Asthma watched as an unbreakable toy tea set of pink plastic was placed in the middle; he was picked up and dropped on one side. Then, the Witch galumphed over, and eased her bulk into a seated position. Sue thought she looked like a vast mound of non-dairy topping.

Asthma began to lick a paw, in an attempt to retain some dignity. He wanted to crawl away somewhere and hide until his fur grew back.

'No, no! You have to just take it! That was our deal,' the Witch said. 'Sags, get Kitty some tea!'

A particularly jowly sag grabbed a teacup and pretended to pour tea into it. 'Do you take milk or lemon?'

Asthma didn't know what to say. Physical pain he could endure; he was an old pro at that by now. But being made to look foolish . . . He was incredibly embarrassed by the whole thing, so embarrassed that he felt he could quite literally die.

Asthma's pause enraged the Wide Witch. 'You're not doing it right! You have to pretend!'

'Sorry,' Asthma said weakly. 'Milk . . . and sugar.' He could barely speak from mortification; the tittering crowd made him feel even worse.

They made an odd couple, the small, bizarrely shorn cat and the blimped-up Witch, who broke scales like so many Christmas crackers. For a few moments they each pantomimed drinking tea, then the Witch picked up an empty plate. 'Sandwich?' she asked.

'No . . . thank you,' Asthma said, swooning. Asthma

had made himself as small as possible. How he longed to escape into the bushes.

The crowd's laughter increased. 'Nice bonnet!' someone yelled. 'Eat him!' another one said – for that was the inevitable conclusion to the scene. Asthma steeled himself. Would it be better to be swallowed whole? He wondered.

'No,' the Wide Witch said, throwing down her paper napkin with rainbows on it. 'This creature is too . . . ridiculous to eat.'

The crowd gasped. Could it be? This demon who had once sucked down an entire jar of mayonnaise in less than fifteen seconds – this eating machine whose gustatory motto was, 'As long as it's died, and fried, it's going inside'—*she* was rejecting Asthma?

As the seconds passed, the crowd's disbelief turned to laughter, a horrible, raucous, jeering sound. But the most horrible thing about it was that it was infectious, and from their vantage point fifty feet away, Sue and Loo had to bite down on sticks to keep from joining in. Asthma wasn't a bad guy, even if he was a little weird, and they didn't want to make him feel any worse. But eventually even Sue and Loo couldn't help it. They knew they shouldn't have, but it's difficult to stand up to a crowd.

His pride shattered, and with the ridiculous clothes

still attached, Asthma finally slunk off into the under-brush.

'There!' the Witch said. 'We won't be seeing him again. Now, let's go and put the rest of the freaks in their place!'

'Oh dear,' Sue said, as the various ululating children of the night, all wearing Blarnia tourism t-shirts, streamed towards them. 'Hide!' she said to Loo, who promptly stood up and started waving her hands.

'Yoo-hoo! I'm over here, evil sort!' Loo called to them, but it was useless. I've told you about Blarnians' poor vision, and even if they could've seen in the predawn gloom, someone had already come up with some great Dead Asthma jokes, and everybody was laughing too loud to hear.

As their dust cloud dissipated, Loo stamped her foot. 'What does a girl have to do to get killed around here?'

CHAPTER 15

 It is true that the Witch's followers were a pretty rough and unattractive lot (so unattractive, in fact, that one wonders just where *they* got off making fun of anyone's appearance). But unfashionable as they might have been, it is distinctly unfair to call them 'rabble' as some have. They simply were not blessed with the same opportunities available to other Blarnians. This did not make them evil. Oh sure, a few were evil, but most were simply doing what their friends were doing — that's just inhuman nature.

But they felt that the rest of Blarnia looked down on them, and they were probably right to some degree. Surely a few of the other Blarnians, especially those trying to explain unfulfilling lives, harboured all sorts of unkind wishes and uncharitable thoughts about the followers of the Wide Witch. That they took all the jobs, that they had too many children, that they weren't *real* Blarnians — it's always the same.

But really, most people in both groups just wanted to get on with life. So it was particularly ironic that the

followers of the Wide Witch had mortified and embarrassed Asthma, who was probably the one person in the
entire fantasy world who would accept everyone just as
the Editor-Behind-the-Scenes made them, even if it
was wall-eyed, festooned with repulsive wens and with
carrion-breath strong enough to burn paper. Everybody else – no matter which side they were on – tended
to walk around feeling like a bit of a loser, sure that
everybody else agreed with them. And when you are
sure someone doesn't like you, it's only natural that you
not like them first.

It was easy for the Wide Witch to play on this for her
own ends. She told them all sorts of lies about the other
Blarnians, how the followers of Asthma ate babies and
did all sorts of disgusting things to each other whenever
it got dark. The Wide Witch's followers had been living
off by themselves for so long that they would believe
almost anything, especially if it came from someone as
large and impressive as the Wide Witch.

The Wide Witch had spent the entire party before
Asthma got there whipping her followers up into a
frenzy. 'We're a peaceful people,' she said. 'We don't
want to fight.'

'So let's not,' a minotaur said.

'That's exactly the kind of attitude that guarantees a
war,' the Wide Witch said. 'Maybe it's the beer,' a
crettin said, 'but I don't think I follow.'

'Weakness! You can never show weakness! They're this close to attacking us as it is!' the Wide Witch said. 'So we've got to attack them first.'

'Let me see if I have this right,' the minotaur said. 'Since we don't want war, we've got to start a war, to make sure one doesn't start. Otherwise, if we don't start a war—'

'There's guaranteed to be one,' the Wide Witch said.

'Wait,' a banshite said, 'aren't we *guaranteed* to have a war if we start one?' The crowd seized upon this point. The Wide Witch cut through the hubbub.

'Look, they want what we have, and they'll take it if we don't stop them.'

'They're welcome to it,' a sag said, holding up the worn hem of her particularly decrepit dress. 'I'd rather go naked.'

A shudder went through the crowd. Then, a fhoul broke in. 'I don't know about the rest of you, but I've actually done pretty well since Asthma's been in town. Before, everything was frozen, but now there's rotting bodies all over the place.'

'You're missing the point!' the Wide Witch said impatiently. 'They want to destroy our entire way of life.'

'What's that even mean?' the sag said.

'All the things we hold profane,' the Witch said,

improvising. She hadn't expected such logical rigour from what were, after all, the unclean. (Not that she was exactly super-fresh herself, especially since it had become hot.) 'Look, there he is!'

Asthma's arrival had saved her from having to explain any further, but now that they were heading towards Asthma's camp and a fight, the Witch's followers were getting less gung-ho by the step. What had seemed like a great idea when they were all sitting around the Stone Bathtub didn't seem so wonderful now. Bathing a cat was one thing, but actually fighting was entirely another. And what was their 'way of life' anyway, except sitting around being scary? And, frankly, everybody was getting pretty sick of that. Ghosts and banshites and crettins are just as scary to each other as they are to humans. What's more, you never got used to it. Just because one is, say, a ghost, that doesn't mean one enjoys constantly fouling one's trousers.

So even if Asthma wanted to change their way of life – which many of them doubted – it might be an improvement. This, plus the natural human reluctance to get beaten up, meant that more and more of the Wide Witch's followers were ditching the whole endeavour and going home to discuss the events of the evening over some beverages of a celebratory nature. Even

those who continued to follow the Wide Witch as she
trundled towards Asthma's camp, began to kick back,
often with the help of various secret caches of intoxicat-
ing this-or-that they had secreted on their undead
persons. The only way the Wide Witch could manage
to get this ever-more-openly partying horde to keep
moving was to tell them (untruthfully, of course) that
there was tons more beer and snacks at Asthma's camp,
all of which would be theirs for the taking.

As the Wide Witch and her followers made their way
towards the camp like a drunken amoeba, Sue and Loo
went off in search of Asthma. Now as anyone who has
ever tried to find a cat can tell you, you find him when
he *wants* to be found, and not a moment sooner.

Unless, of course, he's dead.

They found Asthma under a juniper bush, curled up
so that his tail covered his face. It looked as though he
was covering his eyes to forget what had just taken
place.

'I think he's croaked,' Loo said, reaching for the
shorn and scrawny body.

'How can that be? In spite of what you might think,
Loo, bathing doesn't kill you.'

'I think he died from embarrassment,' she said. 'I
mean, look at him.' The cat did look ridiculous, with his
summer haircut and the dolly clothes.

'Well, if he is dead,' Sue said sternly, 'we must leave him alone. We mustn't ever touch dead things, Mum said.'

'Is Mum here? No, she isn't,' Loo said. She gave Asthma a little poke, feeling envious.

If Loo touched the body, Sue thought, sooner or later Loo's going to touch me, so what's the difference? 'In for a penny, in for a pound' seemed to be the operative rule regarding Death Cooties. She elbowed Loo aside and scooped up the cat.

Loo, ever vigilant for inconsistent standards, exploded. 'Hey! How come you can hold him and I can't even touch him? Just because you're older doesn't mean . . .' Immediately, a spiteful plan blossomed in Loo's brain. She took out the little vial that Father Xmas had given her, then opened it.

The nasty smell reached Sue's nose immediately. 'Whatever you're about to do Loo, don't,' Sue said. 'I'm not kidding.'

'Jerk!' Loo said, and flung the stinky stuff directly at Sue's face. Sue instinctively held the limp cat up to protect herself.

'You're the jerk, you jerk!' Sue hollered. 'Look, you got that smeg all over the cat!' She put the cat down. It remained still.

'I didn't, you did,' Loo said. 'You were the one that held it up!'

'But you were the one that threw the—' Sue saw red, and lunged at her sister. Death for Loo suddenly became quite appealing to Sue, if she were the one doing the honours. The pair struggled, but Sue, being older, soon had the upper hand. Her hands clamped around Loo's throat.

'Yes!' Loo gurgled. 'Do it! Do it!'

At the last moment Sue came to her senses and let go. In the dark underbrush at the edge of the hilltop, the two girls sat, panting.

'Say you're sorry,' Loo said.

'I'm not.'

Incensed, Loo was about to resume battle – then she noticed something. The cat was moving! 'Look!' she said.

Perhaps it was magic, or a trick of the light, but Asthma was most definitely moving. Even more miraculous was that his shaved-off hair was growing back before their very eyes!

Asthma sat up, and began grooming himself furiously. 'Thank you, children,' he said. 'Or should I say, "Thank you, Rogaine"?'

As Asthma's hair returned, so did his energy. 'I don't mind telling you, I was mortified,' he said.

'Did you die?' Sue asked.

'I'd be the last one to know, now wouldn't I?' Asthma said. 'People always talk about "dying from embarrass-ment", but I suppose we see now it can't really kill you!' Asthma batted the fringe on Loo's jacket. The cat was almost giddy with pleasure, a perfectly logical reaction when something you've dreaded turns out not to have been that bad at all.

'But Asthma, what does it mean?' Loo asked.

'You've been in this book long enough to know not to ask questions like that,' Asthma said.

'Don't evade the question,' Sue told the cat, who was vigourously grooming his new fur.

'Then here it is, as best as I can figure it,' Asthma said. 'There is a Cheap Magic, something that gives cheesy books drama. Making a character beloved, then killing it off – that's Cheap Magic. The Wide Witch knew of this. But there is something she did not know about, and that is the Cheaper Magic that requires that Good triumph, Evil be punished, and the audience go home happy. The Editor-Behind-the-Scenes knows everything – therefore, he knows what people like.'

Asthma suddenly flexed all four feet and hopped straight up into the air. He did it four times.

'Why did you do that?' Loo asked.

'No reason, just happiness. I get this way every time,' Asthma confided. 'It's the best feeling in the world. Do you think,' Asthma asked in-between grooming licks, 'do you think there's such a thing as a resurrection addict?'

The girls shrugged. They didn't much care, and frankly, it was getting a little chilly when the wind blew.

'And now,' Asthma said, 'stand back, children. I think I'm going to . . .'

Asthma's body began pulsing and he made weird little back-of-the-throat pukey sounds. Then the girls saw something miraculous, something they'd surely never forget: a three-pound hairball.

Asthma cleared his throat. '*Much* better,' he said. 'Now: catch me if you can!' He bolted off into the undergrowth.

'Oh, for God's sake,' Sue said. 'I want to go home.'

Wearily the girls followed Asthma – or what little they could see of him, there in the dark, mucky forest. Within minutes, they were scratched from branches and bruised from tripping over roots. They called and swore at the cat, but Asthma would not stop. Finally, they found themselves in front of the Wide Witch's castle.

'I've got an idea,' Asthma said. 'I'm the last dude she'll expect to see. Let's sneak in and scare the living heck out of her. How much will you give me if I make her wet herself?'

'Uh, nothing,' Sue said. Asthma seemed a lot more fun-loving since his rebirth, but fun-loving adults made her vaguely uneasy. 'Wait, that's private property!' she said, as the cat took off.

Loo, a few steps behind her sister, stumbled out of the forest. 'I lost my other shoe,' she said.

CHAPTER 16

 Sue and Loo marveled at the figures made of icing. All of them had been frozen just as they had been in the moment the Wide Witch had cast her spell – which meant that, to a one, they were all frozen in vulgar attitudes of profound disrespect. The more demur among them were simply giving rude gestures; those creatures wearing pants had dropped them, to give their adversary the posterior salute.

Many of these bottoms were hardly appetizing under the best of circumstances, but what confronted Sue and Loo was even more nightmarish. Most of them had been badly melted by the sudden warming, and so the majority of the frozen creatures looked like vaguely pornographic candles. The new warmth had also awakened a plague of flies, and they clustered around the buttercream statues like so much body odor.

Asthma made a quick search of the house. 'She's not here,' he said. 'Oh well—it was a nice idea.' He made a move to leave, but Loo's cry stopped him. She had found Mr Dumbness.

'Here he is!' Loo yelled. 'Asthma, Asthma, you must turn him back again! He owes me a mix tape.'

'A what-what?' Asthma asked with bewilderment.

'A mix tape,' Sue explained. 'A homemade collection of songs. Guys usually give 'em to girls they want to—'

'Make him real, Asthma!' Loo said. 'You can change him back again, can't you?'

Asthma hesitated. 'I suppose I could, Loo, but—'

'But nothing! I want my tape!' Loo said, stamping her foot. Recalling all the things she'd been through in Blarnia, it was only understandable that she'd want what she came for.

'But Loo, if I did him, I'd have to do them all,' Asthma said. 'That's only fair.'

'So what else do you have to do at 4:00 am on a Tuesday?' Sue said.

'But – if the Editor-Behind-the-Scenes has them frozen like this, He surely has reasons for making it so. To bring them back to life would—'

'Asthma, if you don't bring my friend back to life, we'll show everybody all the pictures we took of you when they were giving you a bath.' Loo gave her sister a look that said, 'Go along with this, okay?'

Asthma relented – how could he not? But he wasn't happy. 'This never ends well,' he grumbled, padding over to where Loo and Dumbness stood. 'Where are his arms?' Asthma asked Loo rather crossly.

'He had two the last time I saw him,' she said. 'Hurry up and make him alive again.'

'You must lift me up,' Asthma said. 'I must breathe on him.'

Sue thought he must be crazy – maybe the resurrection had scrambled his brains? – but went ahead and picked Asthma up anyway. The cat leaned over until he was nose-to-nose with the Faun, then breathed. Instantly the buttercream icing was replaced by flesh and blood – such as was left.

The Faun awoke with a cough. 'Cat . . . breath,' he sputtered. Then the poor creature yelled, 'Where are my bloody arms? I'm a bloody parapelegic!'

Asthma wasn't surprised in the least. 'You explain it to him, Loo. Sue, come help me do the rest.'

Most of the creatures – even those that didn't look like candles left on a hot radiator – didn't appreciate being brought back to life. 'There I was, in the afterlife, which was bloody nice, you know?' a leopard with melted ears said, as the group walked back to Asthma's camp. 'Not deluxe by any stretch of the imagination, but quiet. Peaceful, like. Superb weather.'

'And so tidy,' a unicorn chimed in. 'Was it tidy, where you were?'

'Oh yes, very,' the leopard said. 'After the initial shock of the change, I must admit I was very happy. I'd made it through all this bollocks, right, and was just settling in for an eternity's bit of rest, and – bango! – Mr Wonderful here drags me back down to this piece of . . .'

'Now, now,' Sue said, 'you should be grateful to be alive.'

'Grateful?' the leopard said, voice rising. 'Grateful? With these melted ears, and this lumbago that I thought I was rid of forever? And my wife? She's around here somewhere, waiting to give me a thrashing. "Honestly, sweetheart, I didn't go and see Darlene, I was frozen, a statue made of buttercream icing!" Like she'll believe that. Yeah, I'm grateful all right. I'm *speechless*.'

Every animal and mythological creature Asthma resurrected had a similarly bad attitude about the experience. By the time the group had reached the Fords of Bazooka, a distinctly ugly mood hung about them like a bad smell.

The scene that greeted them was positive, however. The Wide Witch's followers had always been more interested in celebrating victories than in achieving them, so when it was clear that Asthma's followers did not have loads of free beer, and did not exactly appreciate being woken up by a band of drunken rowdies of the night, most of her minions had exited almost immediately. Those that had stayed did so in the hopes that something in the camp could be magically fermented into alcohol, and so began experimenting with various items fished from the rubbish. Pete and two sags were sitting next to a magical still, chatting amiably as they waited to try homebrew made from a paper napkin.

The Wide Witch was having a rougher time of it, however. The dark and stumbly trip through the forest had resulted in some muck getting into the barrel of her wand, rendering it useless. (A dryad was using it to curl her hair.) And so some of the more fully awake members of Asthma's camp had cornered her in the pavilion. There could be no peace between the Wide Witch and those she wanted to enslave; it had to end here.

Asthma's resurrected army surrounded the pavilion. To a one, they were raring to attack someone, anyone, simply to work off their anger over being back in Blarnia. But Asthma bade them stop. 'No, wait – I want to see if it happens again.'

Inside the pavilion, a gerbil – one of Asthma's would-be surrogates – scurried up the Witch's chest. She hated rodents (especially the poky feeling of their scrabbling feet) but dared do nothing but squirm. The gerbil unsheathed a tiny, useless sword, and the crowd roared its approval.

'I do this in the name of Asthma!' the gerbil yelled.

'Father,' Asthma mumbled, burying his head in his paws. 'Forgive them, for they have totally missed the point . . .'

Just as the gerbil was set to plunge the tiny implement into the Witch's breast, she cried out. 'Wait! Wait! I have something to say . . . As many of you know, I was fortunate enough to spend a lot of time with Asthma, right before he died.'

'Now there's a coincidence!' somebody yelled, but the Witch went on.

'Quiet! This is my big scene!' she bellowed. 'I know I haven't been perfect. I've made some mistakes – we all have.'

'I haven't!' somebody yelled.

'I haven't either!' added another.

'It's like Asthma said, 'Let he who is without sin, cast the first—' The Wide Witch was promptly raked with a hail of pebbles flung from all directions. After it stopped, the Witch was incensed. 'Come on, people,' she said, putting her hands on her hips. 'Don't lie. You, moose: I know what you all do at night. I can hear you clear up in the castle.'

A moose in the crowd blushed.

'And you, macaw. Somebody taught you to talk dirty, and it wasn't me . . . Now, getting back to my big monologue: It's a terrible tragedy that Asthma's shining example of honesty and compassion was snuffed out before its time. Life can be cruel, and so can I. But what's done is done, and we all must work together to make a better world . . . led by me.'

'Boo!' the moose said, trying to get his own back.

'Do you want to do it?' the Wide Witch countered. 'Do you want to run Blarnia?' The moose was silent. The Wide Witch looked down at the gerbil. 'How about you? Do you have what it takes? Do you have the *will*?'

The gerbil dropped his sword, shook his head, and scrambled down the bulging monarch to the ground.

'I thought not . . . No one was more affected by Asthma's death than I was. I'd give anything to have him back here with us, but that's impossible. The only thing left is to carry on living as he would want us to.'

'That's true,' a voice in the crowd muttered. Back, near the apron of the pavilion, Asthma said quietly, 'Here it comes.'

The Wide Witch continued. 'Each of us must ask ourselves, what is the appropriate way to honour Asthma's memory? Is it to slaughter myself and my minions?'

'YES!' several people yelled enthusiastically.

'No,' said the Wide Witch. 'I don't think it is. As we all know, for reasons I don't quite understand, but I'm fairly grateful for now, Asthma's life's work was spreading peace and brotherhood.'

'She's got a point there.' There were murmurs of assent, first grudging, then more wholehearted.

'It's all over,' Asthma whispered, half to himself but loud enough for Sue and Loo to hear.

'So if Asthma were here today, I think he'd say to us, "Don't fight. Life's too short." '

There were real cheers this time.

'And you know what else he'd say?'

'What?' 'Tell us!' She really had them eating out of her hand now.

'He'd say, "Life's also too short to worry about all the complicated things. Let the Wide Witch take care of them – you just do your job . . . collecting pebbles or something, whatever it is you do, and let the Wide Witch handle all the difficult decisions.'

'Sounds good to me!' someone in the crowd said. 'I'm two weeks behind on the pebbles!'

'I haven't got a head for figures anyway,' another person in the crowd added.

'Just do whatever the Wide Witch tells you to.' In fact, I'm *sure* that's what he'd say.'

'Three cheers for the Wide Witch!' someone shouted, and the crowd followed. 'Hip-hip-hurrah! Hip-hip-hurrah! Hip-hip-*hurrah*!'

Loo was trying not to notice the prominent erection on the centaur standing next to her.

'Gross,' Loo said, giggling quietly and elbowing her sister to look.

Sue had no time to giggle. Asthma turned to the girl and began to speak. He wore a sardonic smile, an unsettling expression indeed to find on a cat. 'I keep saying to myself, "This time it will be different. They can't fall for the same transparent trick every single bleeding time." And you know what?'

'They always do?' Sue said, guessing. 'And that's . . . bad?'

Asthma licked his nose, something he often did when he was pleased, and said, 'Sue, that brain of yours isn't half-bad. It isn't half good, either, but you have to start somewhere. Now,' Asthma said, 'lean down.'

Sue did so, and Asthma leaped into her arms. She felt flattered; it was the first time she knew of Asthma letting anyone hold him. She felt less flattered when he climbed from her arms to her shoulder and turned to the crowd; he had just needed more height to make an announcement.

'Blarnians!' Asthma shouted. 'I have returned!'

A few people turned and looked.

'Big deal,' one said. 'You're old news.'

'Yeah,' another said. 'We have to make our way in a post-Asthma world, and I for one frankly don't appreciate you coming back and making it even more confusing.'

'Yeah!' The crowd spoke as one. 'Go away! Be dead again!'

For once, Asthma was at a loss for words. He'd expected at least some enthusiasm.

Loo stepped in. 'Look at all the other ex-dead people we brought back,' she said, pointing at the somewhat worse-for-wear creatures standing outside the pavilion. 'It's a *miracle*!'

'My arms! I lost my arms!' Mr Dumbness yowled.

'Charlene!' a somewhat melty-mouthed ex-statue said, spotting his wife with another dwarf.

'I . . . thought you were dead,' Charlene sputtered lamely. 'What's wrong with your face?'

A young dryad girl scowled, hands on her hips. 'Mum, don't tell me you rented out my room! My stuff had all better be there, or else!'

'You can just go and be dead again,' a Blarnian fairy called to its recently resurrected mate. 'I cashed in your life insurance and I'm not giving it back!'

Even the Wide Witch got into the act. 'I went to a lot

of trouble to kill you all,' she said, 'and I'd appreciate it if you'd have the decency to stay that way!'

Things were about to get very, very ugly, with the resurrected contingent (already quite peeved at being brought back, remember) battling to the death with the people that were none too glad to see them again. Curses were being flung; soon it would be rocks, and then God-knew-what.

Followers, Asthma thought. Nothing good ever comes from having followers. It's even worse if you do what they ask you to. The Editor-Behind-the-Scenes had even told him as much, before he left. 'Just get in and get out,' He had said. 'Don't take sides, or do anybody any favours.' But now, as usual, he was all tangled up.

Asthma leaped from Sue's head, and gave a great yowl, one of those midnight specials that cats make to attract attention – the kind that seem to last for a minute and make your eardrums itch. Everybody stopped shoving each other and looked at the small black cat.

'People, you've simply got to get your act together. I *can't* keep coming back from the dead – the dry cleaners won't take my cheques.' The wisecrack fell on deaf ears, as neither dry cleaners nor cheques existed in Blarnia. 'Tough crowd,' Asthma said. 'The

Editor-Behind-the-Scenes obviously wants you all here, probably so you don't break any of the more expensive worlds. Or maybe he just wants to keep an eye on you. Who knows why? He works in mysterious ways, but at least he's working, and how many of you can say that?

'If someone is driving you crazy, remember: they are just as God made them. Your problem is with the manufacturer. All right, quality has gone down, we'll all admit that – but you simply can't expect the same level of craftsGodship that you had back in the hand-tooled Adam-and-Eve days. The same goes for worlds, too. This one stinks, and if your nose is as sensitive as mine is, you'll know I mean that literally. Nobody in their right mind would choose to be in Blarnia, especially now that we're all knee-deep in mud and decaying badgers.'

'What's your point?' someone called impatiently.

'My point is what it always is,' Asthma said. 'Things are hard enough without everybody going around being beastly to each other.'

'But we *are* beasts,' someone else yelled.

'Not all of you,' Asthma said. 'Some of you are mythological, and others' – he looked at Loo, who smiled – 'well, I don't know what you are, but you can all try a little harder to be nice.'

'See?' the Wide Witch said. 'You heard him. Asthma said everybody should be nice to me, by doing what I say.'

'And *you*,' Asthma said, fixing the Wide Witch with a stern look, 'you need to go into therapy. I don't know if something happened in your childhood or what, but whatever it is it's no excuse to be a blight on the landscape.' Asthma turned back to the crowd, scattered sections of which had begun to tussle one another, the moment he had begun speaking to the Witch. 'If you must fight, I command you to form a Parliament, to cut down on the bloodshed and give the rest of us some solid entertainment.'

Asthma's 'peace-and-brotherhood' gambit went down as well as it always did, which is to say not at all; but the parliament struck everyone as a grand idea, especially those who had realised that they were likely to get the worst of it, if things came to blows. They spent a happy hour choosing sides; the main two parties were the Asthmatics and the Obesitarians, but there were many other, smaller ones like the Apathetics and the Free Radicals, and the Malingerers and the Citizens for Better Upholstery. Soon the hilltop was alive with the happy sounds of bickering and self-righteousness, and before the sun set, Blarnia was undergoing its first-ever constitutional crisis. There had been a motion put forward by the Asthmatics that called for 'an immediate end to all stealing from the human world.' The Obesitarians were determined to fight it. The Apathetics, predictably, didn't care.

CHAPTER 17

 This story is almost over, and thank goodness for that, for I'm sure you're quite as sick of it as I am. But before we part, the Cheaper Magic forces me to answer a few questions.

With the Wide Witch installed as Prime Minister, and the parliament reasonably contentious and non-sensical, all that was left was the crowning of a figurehead – or four figureheads, as the case may be.

'Meet me at Cair Amel,' Asthma told the children the next morning. In a flash of improvised ceremony, fair Blarnia became freighted with four royal layabouts: King Pete and Queen Sue, King Ed and Queen Loo. Now, you might be asking, what did any of them do to prove they could govern a country? And the answer is, nothing, but the Editor-Behind-the-Scenes knows how to flatter His readers. This wasn't such a big deal, for unlike the old days, Kings and Queens don't do much besides snip ceremonial ribbons and take tours of buildings on the very cutting edge of dreadful architecture.

Somehow Blarnia managed to survive the adolescent

hormones of its rulers, who attempted to declare war on each other every time one would enter their bedchamber without knocking, or eat the last bit of ice cream stolen from the human world, or keep making that dorky face even after I asked you not to. In time, Pete, Sue, Ed and Loo turned from irritating, neurotic children into deeply flawed adults.

Since imperious and insane characters tend to blend together, it was difficult for their subjects to tell the four rulers apart. So they gave each monarch a nickname; for example, it was King Pete the Loose Cannon. Queen Sue the Torpid balanced her older brother nicely, restraining his excessive energy and harebrained schemes with a wearisome practicality that drained the will out of all who heard it.

Then there was King Ed the Avaricious.[23] King Ed spent years battling the Blarnians' habit of declaring one commodity as valuable, then changing their minds just as Ed had accumulated a great pile of the first stuff. Finally, there was Queen Loo the Stay Away. As she grew older, her attempts to snuff it became more and

---

[23] Ed finally got his voice-recorder. It was only a wooden facsimile carved by Naomi the Beaver, but by then Ed had spent so long speaking into his index finger that he didn't need the real thing anyway.

more earnest. Further, her years of frustration made her try broader and broader measures, and the toll of innocent bystanders grew to an appalling height. Sadly, prolonged exposure to kibble-smelling Asthma-breath had made her virtually unkillable; and so her existence remained a melancholy roundelay of unsuccessful attempts to end her own life, and increasingly perfunctory apologies for ending others'. People began to avoid her, even her ladies-in-waiting. But who could blame them? It is profoundly unnerving to discover your Queen swinging from the end of a homemade gibbet – that was where Loo 'slept' each night – swearing lustily and asking for help to get down. The solitude and failure only made her more unhappy, and she redoubled her efforts. Poor Loo only broke out of this vicious cycle with the help of drugs, and so she was rechristened Queen Loo the Valium.

One morning well into the Perversies' rule, they were addressing (for the umpteenth time) a certain nauseating necessity.

'I put it to Your Highnesses that you are mortal, and being so, cannot live for ever,' said their Chamberlain, a large tortoise. 'The question of an heir must be resolved.'

'Methinks that by "resolved," thou dost suggest the intertwining of one of us with a foul sibling,' Queen Sue said.

King Pete piped up. 'Verily, the whole prospect makes me once again taste the oily savours of my breakfast.' Now that they were royal, all the children spoke like great Elizabethan twerps. (No one else did, but I suppose they felt they had to, to make up for low-class origins.) It was embarrassing, but they were the monarchs.

'Quick, another subject!' Ed exclaimed. 'Yon greasy tendrils creep into the very precincts of my stiff and sweating tongue!'

Thankfully, before this revolting conversation could continue, the Faun burst into the room. He was much older now; his human half was a bit gouty, and his goat half was even more goaty, and so the whole thing was a bit of a mess. Naomi the beaver had carved him two massive prosthetic arms, which stuck straight out like the wings of a plane.

'Your Majesties – unh! – I bring news. UNH!' His wingspan was too great to get through the door.

'Turn sideways, Dumbness,' Queen Sue suggested, 'and approach the thrones.'

Dumbness stopped straining against the doorframe, retreated, and entered the room side-saddle. 'Of course, how silly of me.' He turned to face the monarchs, and bopped a guardsman in the head with his left arm. 'Oh! Sorry!' He turned to help the fallen guardsman up, but in doing so, his other arm swept a priceless vase off a nearby pedestal. 'Oh damn! I am so sorry, Your Majesties.' A lady-in-waiting emerged with a dustpan. 'Let me help—' Dumbness bent down, and his opposite arm lifted up the voluminous skirts of another lady-in-waiting. She gave a scream, and King Pete grew cross.

'I have never liked you, thou knotty-limbed, ill-moralled pignut. State your news and away, bull's-pizzle.'

'Of course you haven't sire, perfectly understandable, really . . .' Dumbness oozed. 'Your Majesties, the White Stag, Nature's perfect wish-granting machine, has returned to Blarnia. '

King Pete was as usual anxious for a fight, and grasped the threat immediately. 'Dost thou ken what would'st happen if that swaybacked alabaster lice-wagon fell into the clutches of our chalky brethren, the Pallormen? Why, the wishes would gush forth like nether-water from a sot. Methinks they'd tear'st us a new one!'

'Aye, there is truth in that, and this besides,' King Ed said. 'If some knavish coxcomb were to wish for all the florins in the world, do you realise what that would do to inflation?'

Queen Loo made no reply, just watching the scene

unfold with her customary slackened jaw and glassy eye.

'Then 'tis settled,' King Pete said, and the four went off in search of the White Stag. They did not find it, as Parliament had put Dumbness up to a joke; the assembled body laughed more and more uproariously at each successive missive from the confused royals. (It should also be said that agents from Parliament were working in advance of the monarchs, 'seeding' their route with locals bribed to give them more and more absurd information.

'There 'tis!' King Pete said to King Ed, who was busy calculating just how much a stand of old-growth trees would fetch, if they were chopped to pieces and sold to the Pallormen. 'The metal tree the crone spoke of!'

Ed, thoroughly tired of the chase (and half-suspecting a joke), waited for the Queens, who had fallen behind. When she pulled along side Ed, Sue asked, 'Where does our dear spleeny brother go, in such haste?'

'To yon metal tree, crowned with lanterns,' Ed said. 'A crone told us the Stag was conceal'd behind it.'

'Fewmets!' Queen Sue said. 'Never trust a crone.'

King Pete approached the streetlight at full gallop, unsheathed his sword, and dealt the utility pole a mighty blow. The forest was rent with a clang as metal struck metal, and King Pete was knocked off his horse and on to his bottom. The horse kept going.

'We will . . . camp here,' King Pete said, trying to salvage some dignity and failing. He picked up his sword, then ran off in the direction of his steed.

'Shall we ditcheth him?' Queen Loo asked.

'As fair a prospect was never spoken, made fairer still by the fact that we must leave it unexplored. Let us follow,' Ed said. 'It would not do to leave Cair Amel four and return one short, hobbled and ridiculous, like a thrice-pawed prancing cur.'

Tying up their horses, the three trudged in the direction of their brother. Soon, they found a queer feeling coming over them, like they were trapped in a book-ending force greater than they could imagine.

'It is – the work of the Editor-Behind-the-Scenes!' Ed said, as they all turned into the children they had been. Trees changed to hippie garb, Elizabethan verbiage slipped back into casual profanity, and suddenly the four of them were back in the wardrobe, sitting in a puddle of the Dreaded Yellow Peril.

'Where's my sword?' Pete mumbled. 'I was a King . . .'

'Wow!' said Loo. 'That was heavy!'

They could hear Professor Berke pounding on the

doors of the wardrobe. 'I know you're in there, you little freaks! Come out and take your hormones!'

'Oh, no . . .'Sue said. 'All that, for nothing . . .'

A haunted look in his eyes, Ed held up his right index finger and spoke into it. 'Memo to self, re: reality: There is no escape . . . no escape . . .'

POSTSCRIPT

This book first came to me as a series of dreams, during my recovery from a mild case of rabies. Some weeks before it was set to be published, my editor Simon called. 'I have some good news and some bad news,' he said. 'Which would you like first?'

'The bad news,' I replied, wanting to get it over with.

'The copyeditor has found certain . . . similarities . . . between your book and another one, published seventy years ago.'

You could've knocked me over with a feather. 'Wow,' I said, 'what are the odds?'

'It happens,' Simon said. 'The good news is, I think you can sue.'

'No,' I said. 'Let the readers decide. May the best book win.' That's just the kind of guy I am.

'Big of you,' Simon said. 'Anyway, I don't think anyone will notice.'

Since that conversation, I've taken a look at the book Simon mentioned, and it's really nothing like my book at all. There are a few slightly similar things scattered here and there, but nothing major. It's really quite obscure – the only place I could find it was in a big display in the window of my local bookshop. The author (whose name I promptly forgot) is clearly trying to ride the coattails of this book. He's even been able to convince some people in Hollywood to make a quickie movie from *his* book, to try to steal my thunder!

I refuse to get mad about it – publishing can be a sleazy business, and I won't sink to that level. Imagine: this fellow has been setting up his 'sting' for over seventy years! Some people will do anything for money. Not me – no matter how many lemons this fellow chucks at me, I'm determined to make lemonade.

So I've decided to offer one hundred pounds to the first reader that can come up with ten similarities between this book and that other one (assuming you can find a copy!). And they have to be genuine similarities, not bogus stuff like 'Both are made of paper,' or 'Both authors are gits.' All entries should be sent to blarniaprize@gmail.com. In the unlikely event that there is more than one winning entry, I will pick a winner at random from all the entries on 25 December, 2005. The winner's name – and his/her list of similarities – will be posted at www.mikegerber.com. Good luck – I think you'll need it!

ABOUT THE AUTHOR

Generations of readers have been put off by the grubby characters, slapdash plotting, and thimble-brained remorseless pessimism that have made Michael Gerber one of the world's least-loved authors. Children and adults alike revile his old-fashioned brand of immature crap.

It was only late in life that the author began to craft the books that have brought so little pleasure to so few. Self-employed as a professor at a prestigious university, Gerber slowly accreted an amorphous clot of like-minded hoboes, scruffy ill-shaven idlers who shared his contempt for contemporary mores, gainful employment, and basic hygiene. This group – christened 'The Stinklings' by the local constabulary – began meeting at a local bar, where they delighted in assaulting students and tourists alike. (Police in college towns are traditionally lenient, some would say too much so.)

During their Saturday night incarcerations The Stinklings took to reading the latest dreary products of their diseased imaginations aloud. These funk-drenched gatherings redolent of rotting tweed, body odour, and leaky drunk-tank toilets, saw the appearance of some of the world's least-loved works of fantasy. As well as frequent socks in the goolies from inmates unappreciative of Gerber's highly theatrical declamatory style. This involved loud singing, interpretative dance, and a voice that was once compared – unfavourably – to having a wasp trapped in your sinuses.

Emotionally stunted and unable to form the most rudimentary of adult relationships, Gerber turned his sputtering imagination to the *Chronicles of Blarnia*, a series of books set in a wondrous land accessible only by magic furniture. The intersection of interior decorating and the fantastic has always been rich territory, but in the hands of an author as crushingly insipid as Gerber, the Blarnia books soon devolved into nothing more than a way to settle scores, libel perceived rivals, and issue petty complaints to an uncaring universe.

After this protracted literary tantrum, Gerber lived out his life quietly, giving talks to local groups (who did not ask him to come) and corresponding with many people (who did not ask him to write) in some bizarre parody of a sensible adulthood. His struggles with Life's biggest questions – 'If there is a God, why can't He make me taller? And *why do I keep getting socked in the goolies?'* – have been held up by people of faith throughout the world as a shining example of what *not* to do.